I0665435

The Restoration of the Male Ego

Reclaiming our sons
and winning our fathers to Christ

Tim Houston

Houston Publishing

Atlanta, Georgia

Tim Houston/Houston Publishing of Albany Georgia.
Atlanta, Georgia 30096
www.tlhouston.com

Book Layout © 2017 BookDesignTemplates.com

The Restoration of the Male Ego / Tim Houston. – 2nd ed.

ISBN 978-0-9716746-2-2

CONTENTS

The path to guiding our sons and fathers towards a meaningful relationship with Christ is challenging, but attainable. For those engaged in this endeavor, seeking to redeem and restore their sons and fathers, this book serves as a valuable resource. It addresses mothers and ministers, parents and pastors, churches and communities, as well as priests and politicians. It is intended for anyone who observes the struggles of men and seeks effective tools to assist them. Despite its modest size, this book offers profound insight. It provides tools, techniques, knowledge, and empowerment, enabling readers to equip and support others effectively.

While the book's purpose was clear, its title was not. It was not a matter of knowing what I wanted it to be, but rather how to articulate it in a way that made sense. When I wrote down my ideas, the title that emerged was "Men don't need parenting: the art of winning men to Christ and the restoration of the male ego." This seemed like a "long title," and felt more appropriate as the first line of the introduction rather than the book's title.

To avoid distraction, I temporarily set aside the task of finding the right book title and continued writing. However, I did not completely abandon the search for a suitable title. Periodically, I revisited the "long title" to maintain focus on the aim of addressing issues related to reclaiming our sons and encouraging fathers.

The focus of this book is on guiding our sons and fathers toward Christ. Jesus was highly effective in engaging men from all walks of life, regardless of their religious backgrounds. Remarkably, without the use of modern media such as television or social networks, multitudes of men gathered to hear him speak by mountainsides and rivers. His followers spanned a diverse range, including Jews, Gentiles, Pharisees, Sadducees, as well as religious and government leaders, politicians, the wealthy, the poor, and others. These followers accompanied him into deserts and wilderness areas and remained with him up to his crucifixion.

This book aims to provide valuable insights. The journey to reclaiming and restoring our sons and fathers is complex, requiring new tools, skills, and capabilities that may not yet be in your arsenal. This includes understanding how to distinguish between help and enabling. While there is a consensus on the need for assistance for men, there may be differing perspectives on what "help" truly entails. Similar to our natural vision, these distinctions can often be blurred. Help means to providing assistance, whereas enabling involves taking action on behalf of someone else. Help encourages change, while enabling maintains the status quo. Help elevates, whereas enabling keeps one stagnant. Help is constructive, while enabling is counterproductive.

The purpose of this book is to offer practical, spirit-driven solutions for identifying men who are committed to positive change. While many men may express a desire to change, not all are willing to undertake the necessary efforts. Recognizing those who are ready for transformation requires both knowledge and the fortitude to let go of those who are not yet prepared.

In the scriptural reference (John 6:26), when Jesus ceased providing food, many followers departed, but Peter and others remained, acknowledging His words as the path to eternal life. It is my hope that this book will guide you in restoring the male ego, reclaiming our sons, and guiding our fathers towards Christ. May you find fulfillment in your journey through these pages.

Crying Sons and Weeping Fathers

A wise son heeds his father's instruction. (Proverbs 13:1)

My dad, my hero

MY dad, my hero. My father was a significant figure in my life. Even after nearly two decades since his passing, he continues to influence me profoundly. His name was JT, but he was affectionately known as Big Man by his friends and family. Standing just under six feet tall and weighing over 300 pounds, he possessed both physical and emotional magnitude. As a child, I would compare my hands to his and try on his shoes, gauging how much growing I still had to do. I now realize that I still have a great deal of growth ahead of me. He was a man of few words, yet when he spoke, his words commanded attention, much like the EF Hutton commercials of old.

My father had four sons, each of whom he loved dearly. JT Jr., the eldest, inherited my father's temperament and strong will. Wilbert, the second oldest, shared my father's thirst for knowledge. Silas, the youngest, possessed my father's intellect. Then there was me, the second youngest, or the third oldest, depending on the perspective. I inherited my father's rugged good looks, but I often felt uncertain about where I fit into the world.

During our formative years, my father took my brothers and me everywhere with him, expressing his love through actions. In our teenage years, he continued to educate us through both precepts and examples. Not once did he display annoyance at our presence or impatience with our lack of understanding.

My father placed significant importance on the quality of his workmanship and diligently imparted these values to his sons. Despite lacking extensive formal education, he was an expert in manual work. He could fix anything, including cars, trucks, washers, dryers, vacuums, air conditioners, stoves, and refrigerators. If it could be broken, he had the skill to fix it. I vividly remember him instructing me on how to prepare a car for painting. The preparation had to be flawless; even a minor imperfection in the sanding would mar the final paint job. He was not only a master mechanic but also a master teacher.

My father never stopped instructing us. There were numerous responsibilities that he involved my brothers and me in, but personally, masking the car was the most unpleasant task. It required meticulous care and precision to ensure that every item not intended for painting was adequately covered. As a young boy, I did not appreciate the significance of quality in my work, leading me to avoid this tedious task whenever possible. Nonetheless, my father remained undeterred. Through patience, repeated efforts, thorough inspections, and strict discipline, he imparted upon me the importance of achieving excellence from the outset.

I deeply miss my father. Even now, there are moments when I find myself grieving for him. Despite my admiration for him and my desire to emulate his qualities during my upbringing, I did not embody his positive attributes. I sought his approval but attempted to achieve it through minimal effort. I failed to appreciate the principles he endeavored to instill in me. Rather than adhering to my commitments, I used them to evade consequences. Instead of accepting responsibility for my errors, I attributed blame to others. Despite my disregard for his guidance, he kept teaching me.

Crying sons

Maintaining a close relationship with sons in this complex world is challenging, even for an involved father. Nonetheless, my father made considerable efforts to preserve our bond. Despite often feeling disappointed in me, he never disowned me, recognizing my value beyond my current shortcomings. But what constitutes value? Where does it originate? According to the dictionary, value refers to a person's principles or standards of behavior; their assessment of what is significant in life.

My father endeavored to instill his values, principles, and standards within me. At times, his efforts were successful; other times, they were not. There are three specific occasions where these efforts failed to produce the intended results. In each of these situations, I ended up in tears, but not for the reasons one might expect.

When I was around eight years old, I saw my father's coin collection and thought about how I could use it to buy candy. The coin collection included coins of various appearances and sizes, some with packaging and some without. Several coins appeared identical to me, so I decided to take a few of the duplicates, thinking he would not notice the missing ones. I took the coins and sold them to Mr. Blue, my father's friend who lived next door. Mr. Blue gave me some money from his pocket and sent me on my way.

The next day, I saw my dad and Mr. Blue studying their coin collections, which immediately made me aware that I was in big trouble. My father promptly recognized his friend's new coins as part of his own collection. He called me over and questioned where I had got the coins. Out of fear, I falsely claimed that I had found them in the lint catcher of the dryer. However, my father knew that this was not the truth. Eventually, I admitted to taking the coins from his collection. Rather than punishing me severely as I had anticipated, he expressed his disappointment by simply shaking his head and walking away. That night, I felt regret for having let down my hero.

The second incident occurred when I was about 12 years old. My father gifted me a valuable watch, a silver Longines-Wittnauer with a diamond bezel and a silver-plated wristband. I cherished this watch and wore it often. One day, while playing basketball at the park, I removed the watch to prevent any damage and placed it in a secure location within my sight. Periodically, I checked to ensure it was still there. After we finished our game, I collected my things and left, inadvertently leaving the watch behind. Upon realizing my mistake and returning to the park, I discovered that the watch was gone.

I was upset not only about losing the watch but also because I expected my father's disappointment. Predictably, my father noticed the absence of the watch, and disappointingly, I lied and blamed someone else for its disappearance. That evening, I reflected on my actions and cried again, questioning how long my father would tolerate such immature behavior. I resolved to improve, and for a significant period thereafter, I stuck to my commitment.

The third incident occurred when I was 16 years old. My father owned a Ford truck which he valued greatly. It was light green with metal flakes in the paint, white pinstripes, and shiny chrome along both sides. On this day, my father sent me to the auto parts store to retrieve a part he needed. He entrusted his vehicle to my care, recognizing that I was aware of its importance to him.

Although I had some driving experience, I was not proficient at making left turns. The route to the store included two left turns, with the second one crossing a divided highway. During the second left turn, I sideswiped another car and damaged the chrome on the passenger side of the truck. Once more, I lied, and my father recognized my dishonesty. Later that night, I cried again, but this time, only on the inside.

Each incident exposed weaknesses, causing me to resort to lying and crying. I was often saddened by my behavior, but during my teenage years, I did not value honesty. I am not alone. Many individuals, including men today, lie to conceal their imperfections. Rather than confront disappointment, some suppress it or limit their potential because of it. Outwardly, they maintain a tough exterior to avoid scrutiny, which would reveal vulnerabilities.

Some individuals resort to theft to hide their flaws, and in extreme cases, even commit more severe actions, reflecting the proverb "if you lie, you will steal, and if you steal, you will kill." This often occurs when individuals do not confront their truth and accept the consequences of their actions. Personally, I learned that disappointment does not lead to rejection, and despite my flaws, I remained my father's son.

Unfortunately, in some cases, disappointment can lead to being disowned. Moses did not grow up with his biological father, and the man who raised him eventually tried to kill him. Raised as an Egyptian but identifying as Hebrew, Moses faced an identity crisis. He killed an Egyptian after witnessing harm done to a fellow Hebrew. When his adoptive father learned of this, he issued a death sentence, but Moses fled before it could be executed (Exodus 2:15). Pharaoh disowned Moses, impacting both Moses and his family. Out of fear of death, Moses then lived on the other side of the desert for 40 years before reuniting with his family.

Weeping fathers

"So he got up and went to his father. But while he was still a long way off, his father saw him and was filled with compassion for him; he ran to his son, threw his arms around him and kissed him" (Luke 15:20).

Fathers do indeed weep, and I observed my father cry on three distinct occasions. The first instance was when I departed for boot camp; the second was during my inaugural sermon, and the third occurred upon the passing of his mother. Remarkably, two out of these three instances of my father crying were related to me. Moreover, it was surprising that my father's tears were shed due to positive reflections he had about me. I came to understand that despite my flaws, my father recognized my greater potential. Similarly, as my father wept for me, I anticipate that I will one day weep for my sons.

I understand the reasons father's weep. As a father and grandfather, myself, I am now acutely aware of what compels a man to weep openly for his offspring. They weep for the sons they have lost and those they have found. They weep for their sons who achieved their dreams, as well as those who did not. Additionally, I recognize that our silent tears are far more frequent than our public ones. I often ponder how many times my father silently grieved for my brothers and me. In his moments of solitude, how frequently did he have to suppress his tears when contemplating the loss of his own father at a young age? Moreover, I ponder the number of instances my grandfather might have privately wept for him.

Secondly, I understand why sons weep. Their sorrow stems from a father's absence. I miss my father. Until his passing, my dad continually imparted wisdom to me, and now I value every lesson he taught. I hold dear the principles he endeavored to instill in me. I honor my commitments, take ownership of my mistakes, and accept responsibility for my actions. I now drive a Ford truck and own numerous watches.

As I strive to emulate my father, I aim to impart to my sons the principles he instilled in me. Using the tools of his trade and through love, patience, meticulous effort, and firm discipline, I will cultivate his spirit of excellence within them. Furthermore, I will express my emotions openly, with the hope that one day they too will recognize and cherish the values they see in their own children.

Finally, I understand the reason I weep. I grieve for the men who grew up without fathers. Having my father in my life did not prevent me from making mistakes. Even though he was actively involved in my life well into my adulthood, my formative years were riddled by errors and failures. I can only imagine the challenges faced by those who lacked a father figure or had fathers unable to impart valuable guidance. Without paternal leadership, who would serve as their role model? How many lies might these men tell? How many accidents might they cause, or how much property might they steal? I weep for the fatherless men and hope that other men will step forward to be the positive influences they need.

Men to the fatherless

I was blessed to have influential men in my life. Beyond the guidance of my biological father, several other men significantly impacted me. My brother JT blazed his own trail, earning a reputation that often led to me being recognized as JT's little brother. My brother Wilbert provided invaluable life lessons and unwavering support, instilling a strong sense of self-belief in me. Additionally, my younger brother Silas, despite his superior intellect and agility, consistently looked up to me even after an unfortunate incident caused by my actions resulted in a serious leg injury for him.

My uncles also had a significant impact on my life. My uncle Leroy exemplified impeccable style and a commanding presence. With his smooth voice, he affectionately referred to me as "can-cutter," though I am still uncertain of its meaning (yet it still brings a smile). Uncle Junior illustrated the essence of unconditional love for his wife, whom he adored for over 40 years through sickness and health. He continued his devotion to God even after her passing. Uncle JJ, aside from my father, was the strongest man I knew. He addressed me as Nephew and often prepared exotic dishes such as possum, raccoon, rattlesnake, and other unique items. There were various other uncles, both related and unrelated, who influenced my life.

There have been several spiritual leaders who profoundly influenced my life. The Late Pastor HJ Coleman Senior, who guided me from infancy to adulthood, was a powerful preacher embodying God's presence on earth. Pastor John I. Davis Jr., in the early years of my fatherhood, demonstrated what it means to be a man of integrity who leads his family in accordance with the Lord's principles. Apostle Stephen Stallworth served as my mentor and pastor in every respect, and the merits of my ministry today are largely attributable to him.

Pastor Vernell Thomas Sr., who acted as my spiritual father, provided healing during my times of brokenness and revitalized my spirit. My admiration for him is akin to that of a son for his father. Furthermore, Bishop Shelton Bady, a friend and classmate, exemplifies excellence in all his endeavors and continues to mentor me in church growth and personal development.

Lastly, my current Pastor, Dr. Mathew Brown, epitomizes a spiritual giant and is dedicated to bringing God's Kingdom to Community. To these distinguished men and the numerous other spiritual leaders who have imparted wisdom to me, I extend prayers for God's love and blessings upon them and their families. Their efforts have undoubtedly made a lasting impact.

There are numerous friends who have significantly influenced my life, too many to list individually. However, I must highlight a few key individuals. Firstly, my best friend Leo deserves special recognition; his impact on my life is so profound that an entire book would not suffice to detail it all. The lessons he has imparted regarding brotherhood and friendship are invaluable, making him closer to me than any sibling, and someone I trust implicitly.

My cousin, Leroy Houston, exemplifies strength and resilience. Despite being diagnosed with cancer and given a prognosis of six months to live, he persevered for over ten years, steadfast in his faith. Pastor Rick Wood is another important figure, combining administrative expertise with pastoral care and corporate excellence. Apostle Tony Brinson played a pivotal role in my life by aiding my self-discovery, providing support, and motivating me to write my first book. Elder Columbus Smith is admired for his unwavering faith that positively influences those around him, and he also mentored me as the Chaplain for the Minnesota Timberwolves, demonstrating effective ministry to professionals.

To these individuals, along with the countless other friends and family members who have supported me, I extend my heartfelt gratitude.

I included this section at the beginning of this book deliberately because men, regardless of having a father figure, require support from others. Whether you are male or female, as those who have influenced my life, you are making a difference. The restoration of the male ego begins within a man's heart through quiet reflection and recognition of the impact that divine guidance and others have had on his life. Influential individuals have significantly contributed to my development, and I am better as a result. If I weep now, it is with tears of joy, because I am above all men most richly blessed!

Ultimately, I appreciate the presence of my father in my life during my adulthood. My father lost his own father at an early age and experienced many hardships as a result. In his early sixties, he suffered a stroke that significantly impacted his life. He was in a coma for approximately two weeks, and upon regaining consciousness, he shared with me his profound spiritual experience. He recounted how, during moments in his life when he felt alone or had to rely on his own strength to overcome challenges, he realized that God had been present with him.

Throughout the seemingly most difficult times, God revealed to him that He had always been there, providing support and assistance. That day would be no exception, and the son that he had always led would now lead him. Standing by my father's bedside, as his son, and the son of my Heavenly Father, I led him to the Lord and won my father to Christ, and that day, we both cried.

Chapter 1 Summary

Central Thought – Why fathers weep

> *"So he got up and went to his father. But while he was still a long way off, his father saw him and was filled with compassion for him; he ran to his son, threw his arms around him and kissed him."* *(Luke 15:20)*

Key Discussion Points

➤ Fathers weep for their sons and sons weep for their fathers

➤ Father's weep for dreams fulfilled and dreams unfulfilled

➤ Son's weep for fathers absent and fathers present

➤ The presence of a father or a father figure does not mean the absence of flaws or failures

➤ Beyond the father figures, men need others to be heroes in their lives

Action Step

Express your gratitude to the men who have had a positive influence on your life by writing a thank-you letter. If they are living, consider sending the letter to them as they may appreciate hearing your words of thanks. If they are deceased, keep the letter as a personal remembrance for yourself.

Men Don't Need Parenting

All Scripture is breathed out by God and profitable for teaching, for reproof, for correction, and for training in righteousness, that the man of God may be competent, equipped for every good work.

(2 Timothy 3:16-17)

No parental instructions required

When I became a man, I gave up childish ways"
(1 Corinthians 13:11)

It was the summer of 1980 when several of my classmates and I arrived in San Diego, California for Marine Corps boot camp. We reached our destination in the middle of the night, feeling exhausted and sleep-deprived after spending the previous evening awake and enjoying our newfound freedom. However, as soon as the bus came to a halt, the situation changed drastically. Several drill instructors boarded the bus, loudly issuing commands. Within moments, we were standing on yellow footprints outside the bus. The drill instructors continued their directives, informing us that we needed to forget everything our parents had taught us, as those teachings were meant for boys. The Marine Corps, on the other hand, would instruct us in becoming men. To properly address the development of the male identity, it is crucial to eliminate the misconception that men require parenting. This understanding must be clear to all who interact with men.

My drill instructors did not consider that I was an 18-year-old away from home for the first time; they made it clear that they would address only the man in me. With loyalty and discipline as their foundation, the Marines eradicated any notion that men need parenting. During the three months of Marine Corps boot camp, without the support of my parents, I rose before dawn each day, and every moment was filled with responsibility and accountability. My peers and I received instruction from numerous drill instructors on matters our parents never addressed. They taught us how to stand at attention for hours without moving, march with military precision, and understand the importance of making our beds with skill and accuracy. They instilled in us the necessity of facing our fears, leading with distinction, and avoiding excuses. Regardless of our backgrounds, the Marine Corps held us accountable for our actions and spoke only to the man in each of us.

A decade later, I became an instructor at the Marine Corps leadership academy, where I taught corporals and sergeants the principles of leadership. The Non-Commissioned Officer (NCO) leadership academy was a formal military institution and a prerequisite for career advancement. Although these young leaders were no longer undergoing the rigorous conditioning of boot camp, they still needed to demonstrate their capability to lead others effectively and responsibly in hazardous situations. Without parental guidance or peer support, they faced the challenges of my instruction, their own fears, and the demanding environment of Okinawa, Japan. Like my drill instructors, my focus was on addressing the leaders within them.

During my tenure as a leadership instructor, I consistently challenged the notion that men required parenting. My role encompassed that of an instructor, coach, and mentor. I led by example, ensuring that every step I asked them to take was one I had already taken myself. I provided comprehensive instruction on various subjects, from physical exercises like push-ups to tactical skills such as handling hand grenades, small arms, and artillery. Following instruction, they were held accountable for what they had learned.

My responsibilities extended to rescuing individuals lost in the jungle, retrieving those who had fallen from the two-rope bridge and were suspended 100 feet above the ground, and untangling participants who became ensnared during the rappelling exercise. On these occasions, I reverted to a demonstration mode, providing further instruction before asking them to demonstrate their understanding by repeating the exercise. My role was to lead effectively, especially when performance fell short of expectations.

This was all done without the concept of parenting or the belief that I should finish the work that their parents left undone. They were beyond that point. Men need instructions. That is why the Marine Corps calls them "drill instructors" and not "drill parents." For my Marines, I was their instructor who taught them everything and assumed nothing. I respected them as Marines, treated them as Marines, and held them accountable as Marines, and they behaved as Marines. This concept is true for developing men as well. Respect them as men, treat them as men, hold them accountable as men, and they will behave like men.

No benefit in parenting men

To begin with, when I use the term "men don't need parenting," I am referring to the words, techniques, and behaviors that are typically associated with parenting. Parenting, or child rearing, is the process of promoting and supporting the physical, emotional, social, and intellectual development of a child from infancy to adulthood. It encompasses both an attitude and a thought-process, as well as actions. When God created Adam, he was fully grown and ready to assume his role of having dominion over all earthly matters. Given that he still required divine instruction, this guidance could not come from earthly parents. To receive the necessary direction, Adam needed the Master Teacher (God) to instruct him.

Secondly, employing parenting techniques on men is generally ineffective. An immature male may resist such methods, while a mature individual will naturally reject them. It is understandable that sometimes one might inadvertently adopt a "let me tell you "approach when interacting with men. This can occur across various aspects of life, and some might have experienced success with instructing men rather than demonstrating actions. However, it is essential to recognize that treating men in a parental manner has negatively influenced our homes, communities, and churches. Mature men are likely to reject this notion because they seek to act under the guidance and authority of their beliefs, and they rely on spiritual teachings for their personal development.

Finally, it is necessary for all men to transition from parental authority to God's authority. In Luke chapter 14, Jesus communicates to his followers the importance of prioritizing their commitment to Him over their parental ties. Individuals who remain under parental control cannot fully dedicate themselves to divine authority. Jesus advises men to leave their father and mother and unite with their wife. The term "cleave" signifies "to adhere to, stick to, or join with." It represents an exclusive union of two individuals into one entity, which cannot be achieved if parental influence persists. Since his wife was created as a suitable partner, she would accompany him and provide the necessary support he requires at the appropriate times.

Men need boundaries

All men have areas in their development where they may need further guidance. Individuals who may still require development in certain areas benefit from clear boundaries and direction, along with a sense of responsibility and accountability. Boundaries encompass the natural, spiritual, and physical laws that govern behavior. They mark the outer limits of acceptable actions and are essential. Respect for boundaries is crucial as it provides warnings to indicate potential danger. All men require boundaries, regardless of their age, class, or distinction. This should be taught early because a child without boundaries may grow into an adult who does not respect them.

God establishes boundaries to guide mankind. Since men are created in God's image, they possess great power and potential. These boundaries help prevent excessive behavior, such as overindulgence, reckless driving, staying out late, and overspending. Man's nature inclines towards conquest, and without divine laws, a man may engage in harmful actions like killing, stealing, and coveting others' possessions. For Adam, God served as his master teacher, offering the necessary guidance, direction, and correction. To ensure Adam's safety and protection, God placed him in the Garden of Eden, where boundaries, responsibilities, accountability, and consequences were clearly defined.

God's boundaries are established for our safety. Boundaries set forth by divine principles serve to ensure the safety of individuals and are fundamental to the progression of male development. To positively influence men, it is crucial to uphold standards of acceptable behavior. In your personal interactions with men, it is essential to establish clear boundaries that align with both natural and spiritual principles. These boundaries should be supported by divine laws that apply to all those who follow them. They are intended to protect your well-being as well as the well-being of those around you. Men who do not respect these boundaries pose a risk, necessitating societal measures such as incarceration for their containment.

Teach everything, assume nothing

I recall a story about some young individuals who were invited to a formal dinner. They were instructed to adhere to proper etiquette, as the event was described as a "fancy" Sunday dinner. However, upon arrival, they were surprised to find that the dinner setting was far more elaborate than any Sunday dinner they had previously experienced. The table featured at least five forks and various other unfamiliar eating utensils. As each course of the meal progressed, the individuals grew increasingly uncomfortable and self-conscious. They began to suspect that the invitation had been extended merely to ridicule them.

Ultimately, their discomfort led to disruptive behavior. Although the intention behind the invitation was positive, the experience did not yield any constructive outcomes for these young individuals. One might consider how different the outcome could have been if the hosts had not presumed that their guests were knowledgeable about formal dining etiquette.

"Teach everything; assume nothing," is the insightful advice provided to me by my colleague and kindergarten teacher, Darleen Smith. It emphasizes that actions being taught must be repeated until it is evident that they can be performed independently. This approach not only prepares individuals for future tasks but also prevents potential embarrassment. Teaching comprehensively and without assumptions requires both time and patience. It should be conducted without the fear of consequences, as this phase is crucial in the foundational development of young males. Instruction under the threat of punishment proves counterproductive, as individuals learn most effectively when permitted to do so freely. This liberty to make and rectify mistakes is integral to learning responsibility.

Teaching responsibility is essential. It is a fundamental aspect of personal development that goes beyond parental authority. Responsibility is part of the developmental process for males, representing the "let me show you" phase. In the Garden of Eden, God taught Adam about responsibility by instructing him to tend and maintain the garden. He provided Adam with the knowledge needed to fulfill these tasks without imposing consequences. God guided Adam on how and what to prune, the appropriate timing and season for each plant, and the purpose and value of everything in the garden. Whenever Adam encountered something he did not understand, he could seek guidance from God. As stated in James 1:5, "If any of you lacks wisdom, you should ask God, who gives generously to all without finding fault, and it will be given to you."

Responsibility involves assigning tasks that individuals have the ability to perform. It essentially means responding within one's capability. God understood Adam's knowledge limits and only assigned tasks he could manage. Responsibility precedes accountability because an irresponsible person cannot be held accountable. Proverbs 25:19 illustrates that relying on an unreliable person is akin to using a broken tooth or a disjointed foot; it is ineffective. Attempting to hold someone accountable who has not demonstrated responsibility will lead to ineffectiveness and frustration.

Teaching can be time-consuming and challenging. Drill instructors typically do not exhibit frustration because they do not expect learners to master skills immediately. They are trained to repeat actions until lessons are learned and internalized. These lessons, once ingrained, can be retained for decades. For example, the ability to stand at attention with feet at a 45-degree angle and hands positioned along the seamline can remain intact even after many years. Understanding the experience of being judged without proper instruction reinforces the importance of teaching comprehensively and creating an environment where learners can make and correct mistakes. It is crucial to "teach everything and assume nothing" to ensure effective learning.

Even great men need instructions

Now Samuel did not yet know the Lord: The word of the Lord had not yet been revealed to him. A third time the Lord called, "Samuel!"

And Samuel got up and went to Eli and said, "Here I am; you called me." Then Eli realized that the Lord was calling the boy. So Eli told Samuel, "Go and lie down, and if he calls you, say, 'Speak, Lord, for your servant is listening.'" So Samuel went and lay down in his place. The Lord came and stood there, calling as at the other times, "Samuel! Samuel!" Then Samuel said, "Speak, for your servant is listening." (1 Samuel 3:7-10)

The concept of "teaching everything and assuming nothing" should replace the idea that "men need parenting" because everyone needs instructions, regardless of their abilities. Samuel was a prominent prophet with a direct relationship with God, leading the people faithfully. However, he also required mentorship at one point in his life. As a child, Samuel's mother dedicated him to the prophet Eli, and he lived in the temple serving God. When he was called, Samuel did not yet know the Lord, and it was Eli who taught him how to recognize God's voice. Eli advised Samuel to respond with, "Speak, Lord, for your servant hears," when he next heard the "voice" calling his name. Samuel followed Eli's advice and from then on could communicate with God directly. Regardless of one's status, everyone requires guidance.

Firstly, it is fundamental to acknowledge that wisdom and guidance come from God. As stated in Proverbs 2:6, "For the LORD gives wisdom; from His mouth come knowledge and understanding." Jesus

Christ recognized the importance of training for all individuals. To His disciples, He served not only as their Savior but also as their master teacher. Over the span of three years, He consistently instructed them through both principles and examples. The disciples witnessed significant teachings such as the Sermon on the Mount, the Lord's Prayer, and various parables. Additionally, Jesus provided guidance on maintaining humility and avoiding public adulation. He ensured comprehensive instruction for His disciples, leaving no aspect unaddressed. Jesus remains an exemplary figure for teaching and mentorship.

Secondly, it is important to note that God teaches individuals how to respond within the scope of their abilities, which is why it is referred to as "response-ability." While age may influence one's ability to respond, it does not negate the necessity of being taught the appropriate response. Moses was 80 years old when God provided him with instructions on how to lead His people out of Pharaoh's grasp. Similarly, Enoch was 300 years old before he commenced his walk with God, and for the remaining 65 years of his life, God guided him on how to live righteously in a world filled with wickedness. Despite differing opinions, it is evident that no individual is too old to be entrusted with the gift of responsibility.

Thirdly, God provides the most exemplary gifts. As stated in James 1:5 (NLT), "If you need wisdom, ask our generous God, and he will give it to you. He will not rebuke you for asking." Jesus did not criticize his disciples for their lack of knowledge on topics he had not yet taught them. Throughout the scriptures, He corrected their understanding and used their errors as educational moments to impart greater truths. For instance, when they could not exorcise the demonic spirit from the boy, Jesus instructed them on the importance of prayer and fasting. When they aspired to be esteemed by others, He educated them on the value of servitude. In times of fear, He instilled faith, and when faced with mortality, He enlightened them about eternal life.

Next, understanding that responsibility evolves over time is crucial. Each lesson in responsibility varies in duration. The phrase "Do not be weary in well-doing" emphasizes consistency. Time eventually reveals whether a person is responsible or not. If the lesson suits their age and ability, they will learn it. For example, Adam took longer to name the animals than to prune a tree, yet both tasks taught him responsibility. Every task and discipline provide insight into personal development. Ultimately, responsibility leads to accountability.

Finally, we firmly believe that God provides individuals with the necessary tools to perform good deeds. "All Scripture is breathed out by God and profitable for teaching, for reproof, for correction, and for training in righteousness, that the man of God may be competent, equipped for every good work" (2

Timothy 3:16-17). This requires an individual to remain connected to God, as His word is sustenance (Matthew 4:4), and His word is Spirit and life (John 6:63).

This connection is what renders a person competent and equipped for all good works. Through Jesus Christ, God has enabled me to become a better individual, and I continue to grow daily in the knowledge of God. Because of my ongoing relationship with Him, I am strong in the Lord and in the power of His might, and I have a clear understanding of God's desires for my actions. Recognizing that men do not require parenting, God has transformed my role from being a drill instructor to being a God-instructor who imparts comprehensive teachings and leaves nothing assumed.

Chapter 2 Summary

Central Thought – No parental instructions required

When I became a man, I gave up childish ways"
(1 Corinthians 13:11)

Key Discussion Points

➢ To instill responsibility, we need to teach everything and assume nothing

➢ Responsibility – let me show you

➢ Accountability – let you show me

➢ The prophet Samuel is a perfect example that even great men need instructions

➢ There is no benefit in parenting men because irresponsible men will reject it and real men will ignore it

Action Step

Over the next three weeks, make a deliberate effort to replace the phrase "let me tell you" with the action-oriented phrase "let me show you." Maintain a log to record occurrences and responses. This log will serve as a visual reminder of the positive impact this change can have on your interactions with men and young men.

Drop the Boy
Cripple the Man

But as she hurried away, she dropped him, and he became crippled. (2 Samuel 4:4 NLT)

When I was a child

"When I was a child, I spoke like a child, I thought like a child, I reasoned like a child" (1 Corinthians 13:11)

W hen I was a child, my parents demanded that we learn responsibility at an early age so that we would not grow into irresponsible adults. They believed that carrying a child constantly would hinder their ability to walk independently, and if you carry a 5-year-old boy, you might end up carrying the 55-year-old man. Miphibosheth, King Saul's grandson, was dropped by his nurse at five years old despite being able to walk. This decision impacted his life significantly. My

31

parents were determined not to carry us once we could walk on our own.

When I was about nine years old, my mom started taking my siblings and me to work in the fields. The field was a farm in rural Michigan owned by a man named Mr. Clarence. During the summer months, we worked the fields to earn money for the upcoming school year. Our responsibilities included harvesting cucumbers, peppers, beans, and tomatoes. Despite the variety of tasks, the workdays were consistently long and challenging. Each morning before sunrise, we would leave home and return around sunset. After eating, we would go to bed and repeat the routine the next day. This experience taught me the value of hard work.

"Hard work never hurt nobody," was a saying my mother often used. She believed a job could only be replaced by another job. At the age of 12, I started delivering newspapers. This responsibility required seven-day-a-week, year-round delivery, with papers due by 5:00 PM on weekdays and before 8:00 AM on weekends. Additionally, I collected payments and reconciled balances owed to the newspaper. I managed these tasks independently, as my parents had taught me how to use my abilities to earn money. I was also elated to finish working in Mr. Clarence's field.

I held several jobs before graduating high school and leaving for boot camp, all of which required responsibility and accountability. My parents taught me the value of hard work at a young age, believing that I could be held accountable as I matured into adulthood. Although I understood this, there were times when I acted irresponsibly. Responsibility and accountability are not fixed traits and can fluctuate based on one's proximity to their mentors. Even as a teenager, I had the autonomy to act against my parents' instructions, typically doing so away from their presence and the principles they taught me.

Reflecting on my growth into adulthood helped me understand Adam's fall. Despite God's guidance, Adam made choices that led him astray. This raises concern for humanity's hope if even Adam faltered in God's presence. Ultimately, everyone must take responsibility for their actions. Thankfully, Jesus completed God's redemption plan for all, but personal accountability is essential before redemption can occur.

From responsibility to accountability

In the previous chapter, we discussed responsibility and its significance. Accountability is the subsequent concept. It represents the phase of demonstrating one's ability to take responsibility. Because Adam maintained the garden effectively, he showed himself responsible and was prepared for accountability. God explained to Adam about the tree of knowledge of good and evil, its location, and how to distinguish it from other trees. He took him around the garden, showing him the trees he could freely eat from. Then, God provided Adam with the commandment and its consequence: "the day you eat from this tree, you will surely die." Accountability involves higher standards as it includes consequences.

Accountability is a higher standard that is inherently linked to responsibility, as accountability necessitates that an individual first demonstrates their ability to be responsible. This expectation cannot merely be assumed. As stated in Luke 12:48, "From everyone who has been given much, much will be demanded; and from the one who has been entrusted with much, much more will be asked." Jesus conveyed this principle through the parable of the talents. In this narrative, the master was aware of each servant's capacity to respond effectively, and accordingly distributed talents (money) based on each servant's ability. One received five talents, another three, and the third, one.

In the parable, after the master instructed his servants on how to handle their talents, he departed for a period of time. Upon his return, he required them to provide an account of their actions. The first two servants, who had received three and five talents respectively, utilized their talents effectively and doubled the amounts they were given, demonstrating responsibility and reliability. However, the third servant concealed his talent and offered excuses for his lack of action, revealing irresponsibility. Consequently, his single talent was taken away and given to the servant who would use it most efficiently.

Secondly, accountability is a fundamental requirement. Saul's lack of responsibility displeased God and deeply affected Samuel, his spiritual mentor. As stated in 1 Samuel 15:10-11, "Then the Lord said to Samuel, I regret that I have made Saul king, for he has not been loyal to me and has refused to obey my command. Samuel was so profoundly moved by this that he cried out to the Lord all night." Similarly, just as my father expressed sorrow during my moments of failure, Samuel interceded on Saul's behalf. Ultimately, due to Saul's disobedience, God removed the kingdom from him and bestowed it upon David, who was known to be a person after God's own heart. Trusting in David's integrity, God was confident in David's ability to manage the kingdom and its associated responsibilities.

Accountability should be established from the outset. King Saul was appointed without demonstrating his responsibility, due to the people's choice based on his physical stature. This approach proved ineffective as accountability requires a foundation in responsibility. When the moment arrived for Saul to fulfill his duties as king, he avoided them. Later, when questioned about his decision to keep livestock that had been ordered destroyed, he blamed others. "And Saul said, they have brought them from the Amalekites: for the people spared the best of the sheep and of the oxen, to sacrifice unto the LORD thy God;" (1 Samuel 15:15 KJV).

Accountability requires understanding an individual's abilities. This understanding negates a uniform approach to development. It is difficult to maximize someone's potential without knowing them well. There is no universal method that suits everyone. Before holding someone accountable, it is important to learn about their abilities. This understanding is developed during the phase where responsibilities are demonstrated. As you teach them different tasks, you also gain insight into their capabilities and limitations. During my time as a Marine leadership instructor, I identified each Marine's strengths and used this knowledge to assign tasks according to their specific abilities.

Finally, accountability involves individuals being required to provide an account of their actions. The Bible indicates that when much is given, much is expected in return. Some individuals, like the unfaithful servant in Jesus's parable, are not prepared to provide an account. In the parable, the man who was faithful over a few things demonstrated that he could be trusted with more significant responsibilities. Conversely, the unfaithful servant, who could not be trusted with even the little he had, saw it taken away from him. This illustrates the consequences of one's choices. All individuals must provide an account, and this account must include repercussions for their actions, as accountability without consequences is not true accountability.

Dropped boys and crippled men

Saul's son Jonathan had a son named Mephibosheth, who was crippled as a child. He was five years old when the report came from Jezreel that Saul and Jonathan had been killed in battle. When the child's nurse heard the news, she picked him up and fled. But as she hurried away, she dropped him, and he became crippled. (2 Samuel 4:4 NLT)

Mephibosheth was not born crippled. When he was five, he was accidentally dropped, resulting in lifelong disability. On the same day, his father and grandfather died in battle, putting his life at risk. Though his nurse tried to protect him, she dropped him in her haste, severely wounding his spirit. The dropped boy became a crippled man. This mishap reflects many men today who have been unintentionally harmed by caregivers. For Mephibosheth, that incident changed his life forever.

Life's journey is rarely linear. Despite our best efforts to maintain responsibility and accountability, unexpected events occur. At various stages in life, individuals will experience interruptions. However, if these interruptions happen before reaching the age of accountability, it poses significant challenges regarding expectations of responsibility and accountability. These individuals may struggle to overcome early childhood deficiencies and discover their life's purpose if they lack foundational guidance. To address these critical issues and gain insights, we need to examine the life of Mephibosheth more closely.

Regrettably, being dropped was not the only adverse event that befell Mephibosheth that day. The demise of his father ended his right to ascend to the throne, and the passing of his grandfather, the reigning king, removed his access to the palace and the princely lifestyle he once enjoyed. Their deaths continued to negatively impact his life, as he no longer had their protection against those who might wish him harm. Similarly, the absence of fathers today continues to have detrimental effects on the lives of boys and men. Fatherless boys grow up to become fatherless men, and without paternal protection, these boys are exposed to risks. Many resort to joining gangs, bearing arms, or other extreme measures to safeguard themselves.

Mephibosheth became fatherless, and his nurse feared for his life. In her haste to protect him, she accidentally dropped him—a tragedy compounding another. Can a man recover if he was unprotected as a boy? How can he become whole without a father figure? Men today grapple with these questions, feeling the continued absence of their fathers as being repeatedly "dropped."

The incident that led to Mephibosheth's injury drastically altered his life's trajectory. On that fateful day, he not only lost his father and grandfather but also sustained injuries that rendered him unable to use his legs. Consequently, he faced the limitation of never being able to stand, walk, or run again. This tragic event marked the beginning of his life as a person with disabilities. From that moment on, his physical condition served as a constant reminder of the accident.

Mephibosheth's aspirations were significantly constrained by this experience, leading to a diminished spirit. Regrettably, the boy who was once full of potential grew into a man defined by his physical limitations. Eventually, Mephibosheth resided in Lo-Debar, a place often associated with the loss of hope and dreams.

From Lo-Debar to the king's table

Then the king summoned Ziba, Saul's steward, and said to him, "I have given your master's grandson everything that belonged to Saul and his family. You and your sons and your servants are to farm the land for him and bring in the crops, so that your master's grandson may be provided for. And Mephibosheth, grandson of your master, will always eat at my table." (Now Ziba had fifteen sons and twenty servants.) Then

> *Ziba said to the king, "Your servant will do*
> *whatever my lord the king commands his servant*
> *to do." <u>So Mephibosheth ate at David's table</u>*
> *<u>like one of the king's sons.</u> (2 Samuel 9:9-13)*

Although Mephibosheth was once dropped, he was not forgotten. Mephibosheth resided in Lo-Debar, an Old Testament town in Gilead known for its meaning "no word" or "no communication." For him, being in such a place likely felt like a final destination, but this was not the case. King David, seeking to honor someone from King Saul's lineage for Jonathan's sake, learned that Saul's grandson, Mephibosheth, was still alive. Despite being informed of Mephibosheth's disability, David sent for him nonetheless.

Unbeknownst to Mephibosheth, he would become the beneficiary of his late father's blessing. As stated in 1 Samuel 20:42, "Jonathan said to David, 'Go in peace, for we have sworn friendship with each other in the name of the Lord, saying the Lord is witness between you and me, and between your descendants and my descendants forever.'"

Jonathan was David's closest friend long before David became king. When David was serving King Saul, Prince Jonathan showed him favor. On multiple occasions, he warned David about his father's intentions to kill him. Jonathan blessed David, and consequently, David later blessed Jonathan's son, Mephibosheth. Essentially, Jonathan created blessings for Mephibosheth through his faith. He blessed David before Mephibosheth was born, and David blessed Mephibosheth long after Jonathan had passed away. Jonathan's faith served as a spiritual legacy for his children. This demonstrates a spiritual truth: if the sins of the father can be transmitted to the children, how much more so can the father's blessings!

Due to his promise to Jonathan, David summoned Mephibosheth and bestowed blessings upon him. King David allocated all the land that had previously belonged to Mephibosheth's grandfather. Additionally, he assigned Ziba, Saul's former servant, along with Ziba's 15 sons and 20 servants, to serve Mephibosheth. From that day onwards, Mephibosheth dined at David's table as one of the king's sons, ensuring he would never have to concern himself with food or shelter again. God delivered him from his "Lo Debar" experience. This serves as an encouragement for men today, as the absence of biological fathers does not equate to the absence of our Heavenly Father.

There is hope for those who feel abandoned. Being troubled in youth doesn't mean a troubled adulthood. We all face hardships, but God places people in our lives to help us. Through Jesus Christ, we're invited to enjoy blessings. As Psalm 23 states, "You prepare a table before me... my cup overflows. Surely goodness and mercy will follow me... and I will dwell in the house of the LORD forever." From Lo-Debar to the king's table: life interrupted no more!

Chapter 3 Summary

Central Thought – Mephibosheth ate at David's
table like one of the king's sons

...she dropped him, and he became crippled.
(2 Samuel 4:4 NLT)

Key Discussion Points

➢ Responsibility and accountability are required for
manhood

➢ Responsibility – let me show you

➢ Accountability – let you show me

➢ Fathers and father figures are needed to prevent
fatherless boys from becoming fatherless men

➢ God can take men from their Lo-Debar (broken
dreams) to the kings table (dreams fulfilled)

Action Step

Pay it forward. Identify an individual, particularly a
man or young man in your community, whose
aspirations have been shattered. Develop a
comprehensive plan to assist him or direct him to
someone who can help rejuvenate his ambitions.
Provide continuous support and encouragement to
prevent him from falling back into despair. Once he has
achieved his goals, encourage him to extend the same
assistance to others.

The Death of the Lion

The lion which is mightiest among beasts and does not turn back before any." (Proverbs 30:30 ESV)

The king of the jungle

I woke one morning with an interesting question from God on my heart. He asked why the lion is called the king of the jungle. It wasn't easy to answer, as the lion isn't the biggest, fastest, or strongest animal. Lions sleep up to 16 hours a day, live in prides, and are more family-oriented than other big cats. None of these traits explain why they are considered kings.

Eventually, I found clarity when God answered my question. He revealed that the lion is considered the king of the jungle because it is inherently born to be a ruler. The lion has no natural predators, allowing it to navigate the jungle with confidence and freedom. Other animals, regardless of size, recognize its presence and respect its power. As Proverbs 30:30

(ESV) states, "the lion, which is mightiest among beasts and does not turn back before any." Furthermore, Psalms 104:21 indicates that young lions roar for their prey and seek their food from God. The bond between the lion and God extends beyond sustenance, as Jesus is designated as the Lion of the tribe of Judah (Revelation 5:5).

The roar of an adult male lion is the most powerful among all roars, audible up to five miles away. Unlike juvenile lions, adult males do not roar for food or following a kill, as they avoid alerting other animals to their presence. Instead, the lion's roar serves to assert his dominance and delineate his territory, which can span up to 100 square miles. Additionally, the roar functions as a means of communication with other lions within the territory. This behavior typically occurs before sunrise and at sunset, rather than during midday, to prevent startling prey.

A lion in captivity does not roar. Unlike a lion in the wild, the lion in the zoo remains silent because his natural territory is gone, and he lacks both literal and figurative pride. This lion has been subdued, and his sense of self diminished. Outwardly, he appears as a lion, but inwardly, his essence as a king is lost, making him a mere shadow of his former self. The circus lion faces even greater indignity, compelled to perform for spectators' entertainment. At the snap of a whip or a gestured command, he rolls, jumps, and sits on demand. While he is inherently a king, the lion within him is subdued, his pride removed, leaving him in silence at sunrise and sunset.

A godly man can be compared to a lion. Proverbs 28:1 states that the righteous are as bold as a lion. When a man is in right standing with God, his confidence and self-esteem remain intact, and he considers the entire kingdom of God as his domain. This individual does not need to assert his dominance vocally because his strength lies in his faith, and he understands that his power comes from his connection to God. Such a man can be likened to Benaiah, who pursued and killed a lion in a pit on a snowy day, Samson, who defeated a lion with his bare hands, or David, who killed a lion as a young boy. The godly man is esteemed in God's kingdom, and as long as he maintains his connection to God, he remains undefeatable.

The destruction of the male ego

For as in Adam all die, so in Christ all will be made alive. (1 Corinthians 15:22)

When God said, "and let him (man) have dominion over everything," He established man's authority and governance. Through this declaration, Adam assumed rulership over the earthly domain. The Bible informs us that Adam's transgression adversely affected all subsequent generations, though this was not always the case. During the period when Adam was in harmony with God, there was peace on earth. The garden thrived under his stewardship, and predators and prey coexisted peacefully. Death and sorrow were absent because both Adam and his environment prospered under his rule.

Adam ruled the earth until he sinned, becoming self-reliant and causing everything to suffer. The ground produced thorns, lambs became prey, and humans began to die. Mankind went from dominion over the earth to struggling under its weight, with Adam now subject to his environment and ego, working by the sweat of his brow.

Adam lost access to the Garden of Eden and had to live in a world he created. Men today do the same, living in human-made environments and ignoring God's spiritual kingdom offered by Jesus Christ. They prioritize worldly gain over their souls, influenced by ego-driven choices. This trap is challenging to avoid as it appeals to man's vanity.

A man's inner self, including his emotions, feelings, and ego, can be manipulated against him. All stimuli that a man encounters—what he hears, sees, touches, or smells—are often designed to boost his ego and subdue his innate strength. As identified in 1 John 2:16, "For everything in the world—the lust of the flesh, the lust of the eyes, and the pride of life—comes not from the Father but from the world."

Negative influences act within a man's subconscious, either affirming him with phrases like "You are the man" or undermining him with statements such as "You call yourself a man." These manipulations, whether inflating or deflating his ego, aim to disrupt his relationship with God. Consequently, the man may become overly self-confident or deeply insecure, ultimately shifting his focus away from God and onto himself.

Sin ultimately led to Adam's downfall. Romans 7:11 states, "For sin, seizing the opportunity afforded by the commandment, deceived me, and through the commandment put me to death." Adam's ego was destroyed because he chose to listen to the serpent over God. With his wife's support, he ate from the forbidden tree, taming his inner lion and killing his kingly spirit. Now master of his fate but lacking confidence before God, he left the Garden of Eden and his fellowship with God.

Man's connection to God, the source of his life

"No man is an island; entire of itself, every man is a piece of the continent, a part of the main. If a clod be washed away by the sea, Europe is the less, as well as if a promontory were, as well as if a manor of thy friend's or of thine own were: any man's death diminishes me, because I am involved in mankind, and therefore never send

to know for whom the bells tolls; it tolls for thee." (From whom the bell tolls – John Donne 1572 –1631)

A devout man must maintain his connection to God, as separation from Him is a prelude to the erosion of the male identity and the diminishing of one's inner strength. This underscores the sentiment that no individual is truly self-sufficient. Although John Donne's words, penned over 400 years ago, remain poignant today: no man is an island entire of itself. As long as one remains connected to the greater whole, their existence will be stable because God is steadfast and unchanging. God is the constant; He is the foundation upon which stability rests, and if a man continues to abide in Him, he holds dominion over all aspects of life. Conversely, if a man considers himself the central figure, he will inevitably sever his connection with God, leading to isolation and eventual downfall.

Adam and Eve serve as a case study in the consequences of a broken connection to God. After being deceived by the devil into disobeying God's command, they lost their spiritual relationship with Him. In an attempt to hide from God's presence due to embarrassment, Adam and Eve covered themselves with fig leaves. Subsequently, this led to blame ("the devil made me do it") and eventual suffering as God issued punishment for their transgression. Analogous to flowers removed from their source of life, Adam began to experience mortality from the day he was expelled from God's presence. The biblical reference, John 10:10, states, "The thief comes only to steal and kill and destroy," indicating Satan's intentions to undermine man's integrity, sever his bond with God, and ultimately bring about his death.

The relationship between man and God is fundamental to his existence, maintaining both his inner strength and ego. When man's ego dominates, the presence of God becomes burdensome, leading to a deterioration of their relationship and instilling fear. Adam's shame over his nakedness diminished his confidence to stand before God, causing him to hide. Conversely, when man controls his ego, he fosters a strong bond with God, allowing him to walk confidently in divine presence. Adam's need to conceal himself from God underscored the real issue: the inadequacy of his relationship with God, not the magnitude of his ego.

Ultimately, Satan successfully implemented his plan to undermine the male ego. He understood that the desire to be like God would lead to an inflated ego, as this was the very reason for his expulsion from heaven. At the beginning of time, he misrepresented God's truth by convincing Adam and Eve that they would not die if they ate the forbidden fruit. He then sought to elevate Adam's ego by suggesting that he would gain wisdom comparable to God's. Any influence that causes a man to consider himself equal to God invariably leads to separation and spiritual death. Satan recognized that man's unwavering confidence in God was a strength, and through deception, aimed to transform it into a weakness. The male ego has been under continuous attack since that time.

Destroyed by misinformation

The serpent beguiled me (Genesis 3:13)

Satan tricked Adam. If God-information is powerful, then misinformation can be equally as powerful. Adam and Eve's relationship with God was destroyed by misinformation. Satan seized the opportunity to distort the commandment that Adam received directly from God. Because the Bible tells us that Eve was deceived first, Adam had a brief chance to reflect, but regrettably, he did not use his time to challenge the source of information. This is a must for a man to say in the right relationship with God because he must reconcile the information received with the word of God. This reconciliation will reveal the real source of information. If a man finds the true source of his information is the streets, social media, or the devil himself, he must recognize it as misinformation and reject it.

Man is accountable to God for his family's spiritual well-being, including the husband-wife relationship. In

Genesis 3:6-7, nothing happened when Eve ate the fruit, but when Adam did, both their eyes were opened. This highlights man's role in protecting his family (Ezekiel 22:30). Ephesians 5:23 states the husband is the head of the wife, as Christ is the head of the church. As the spiritual leader, a man must seek God's guidance for his household, a responsibility he cannot pass on.

Misinformation is most powerful when a person is not connected to God, who provides divine instruction. This instruction forms the armor of God, enabling one to resist the devil's tricks (Ephesians 6:11). God's armor protects against all enemies, seen and unseen, including Satan, the father of lies (John 8:44). Satan distorted God's commandment to exploit Adam and Eve's desire for forbidden fruit. Desire is natural, but we must remember that it comes at a cost.

While Adam was disobedient, he was not blindly deceived. He received the commandment directly from God and had firsthand knowledge of the consequences of Eve's desire to consume the fruit. Instead of confronting the devil or expelling him, Adam chose to follow Eve's lead despite being aware that it contradicted God's instructions. When a man disregards the word of God, adverse effects ensue for everyone.

As a result of Adam's actions, the ground was cursed, yielding thorns and thistles; man would toil with great effort, and death entered the world. Eve also experienced pain, leading to all women enduring painful childbirth (Genesis 3:16-19). There is hope, as the most effective defense against misinformation is the word of God, which serves as a lamp to one's feet and a light to one's path (Psalms 119:105).

Restored by God-information

God-information is the just-in-time directions that comes from God that leads to victory. "But thanks be to God, who gives us the victory through our Lord Jesus Christ!" (1 Corinthians 15:57). God wants all men to live in victory, but men today must be watchful and vigilant. Satan was kicked out of heaven, and he is on a mission to destroy man. Revelation 12:12 says, "Woe to the inhabitants of the earth for the devil is come down to you." All men must guard against the attack of the devil because this attack is to tempt men with sin, knowing that sin leads to spiritual, emotional, and physical death. God-information is the process for a man to get his ego reestablished and to become victorious over the devil.

To do this, man must first acknowledge that he alone is responsible for his choices. This is a prerequisite because God-information is what keeps a man safe. Before Adam fell to Satan's deception, he was still the ruler of his environment, and he had the power to resist the devil. Without checking with God, Adam followed Satan's lead, and he unknowingly became a servant to him. "For to whom you yield your members, you become a servant" (Roman 6:16).

The bible is full of men whose egos and choices led them astray, Nimrod, Pharaoh, Nebuchadnezzar, Herod the great, and many unnamed others. These men, seduced by power and the devil, rejected God-information. Because they were ruled by their egos, they ultimately made choices that were contrary to God, and this was their downfall.

Godly choices begin with faith, and faith in God keeps a man from falling. Jesus instructs all men to have faith in God (Mark 11:22), and sin is the result of the absence of faith. "Everything that does not come from faith is sin" (Romans 14:23 NIV). Faith in God is man's protection against his own choices, and the godly choices are what causes a man to be full of the power of God.

Abel, Enoch, Noah, Abraham, Moses, David, Joseph, Daniel, and many other heroes of faith were perfect examples of what happens when a man's confidence is in God and not himself. "This is the victory that has overcome the world, even our faith. Who is it that overcomes the world? Only the one who believes that Jesus is the Son of God" (1 John 5:4-5).

Faith in God makes a man fearless, though not perfect. Godly choices do not mean perfection because all men are a work in progress. The heroes of faith were courageous men who believed God and took actions that were consistent with His Word, and their faith in God was accounted to them for righteousness (Galatians 3:6). A man's faith makes him righteous, and because it cultivates his connection to God, it keeps him in the presence of God. The presence of God is where true victory resides, but there is still one more enemy that needs to be defeated.

Empowered by God-confidence

"The last enemy to be destroyed is death" (1 Corinthians 15:26). The fear of death immobilized the entire army of Israel. For these men, the prospect of facing Goliath meant certain destruction. Despite his youth, David's confidence in God provided him with a different perspective. David's trust in God was bolstered by his self-confidence, enabling him to recognize that he was greater than Goliath. It was his faith in God that kept him humble. "David said to the Philistine, you come against me with sword and spear and javelin, but I come against you in the name of the LORD Almighty, the God of the armies of Israel, whom you have defied" (1 Samuel 17:45). Overcoming the fear of death is achieved through a man's faith in God.

Jesus removed the fear associated with death through His death, burial, and resurrection, thereby rendering death powerless over believers. Daniel was courageous in defying a law that prohibited prayer, confident in his identity in God. The three Hebrew boys displayed bravery by refusing to bow to a tyrant's demands, even when faced with death in a fiery furnace, asserting their unwavering belief in an omnipotent God. This theme of faith-driven courage continues with Joseph, who was unafraid to embrace his lofty dreams despite being cast into a pit and left for dead by his brothers. Joseph's steadfast confidence in God enabled him to continue dreaming.

Fearlessness alone is insufficient because ego can lead to destruction. Believing oneself to be the source of all good is misguided. The rich man in Luke 12 died on the night he failed to acknowledge God as the source of his blessings. The Bible states, "Every good and perfect gift is from God" (James 1:17). It is unwise to ignore God's role in our success.

"In all thy ways acknowledge him, and he shall direct thy paths" (Proverbs 3:6). A man must take the direct actions needed to stay connected to God. He must believe in his heart that God has given him the victory over the world through his faith (1 John 4:5). If a man does not stay connected to God, the destruction of the male ego is inevitable. This disconnection leads to failure, and the realization that he has failed God leaves the man feeling depressed and defeated. Men in this type of situation often throw up their hands and give totally over to the sin nature. Their heart becomes hardened, and the word of God is left by the wayside. Uncovered, they become victim to the tricks of the devil.

*"I have stored what you have said in my heart,
so I that won't sin against you" (Psalm 119:11)*

Misinformation harms, but information from God heals. To achieve victory, one must seek guidance from God and maintain a strong connection with Him. Faith is essential for finding God's confidence, which leads to triumph. One must actively pursue God, admitting their dependence and approaching Him with confidence, knowing He rewards persistence. As Jesus said, "The Spirit gives life; the flesh counts for nothing. The words I have spoken to you are full of the Spirit and life" (John 6:63). True restoration of the male ego begins and ends with Christ.

Chapter 4 Summary

Central Thought – Man's connection to God is the source of his life

The righteous are as bold as a lion. (Proverbs 28:1)

Key Discussion Points

➢ When a man disconnects from God, his ego is destroyed, and his fearless confidence in God is lost

➢ This man has lost his place in the kingdom, and like a caged lion does not roar

➢ Reconnection to God restores a man's God-confidence and gives him access to God-information

➢ Always challenge the source of the information you receive to ensure its origin is God

➢ Misinformation destroys, but God-information restores

Action Step

Create a habit of questioning the information that you collect. With the advent of social media, competing news cycles, and the bombardment of misinformation, the need to challenge the information we receive is paramount. If the source of your information does not trace back to God, the word of God, the Holy Spirit, or godly principles, reject it.

The Restoration of the Male Ego

And on His robe and on His thigh He has a name written, "KING OF KINGS, AND LORD OF LORDS." (Revelation 19:16)

The Internal Factor: The *David Principle (P1)*

Though an army besiege me, my heart will not fear; though war break out against me, even then I will be confident. (Psalms 27:3)

The *David Principle* states that God's presence within man makes him great. "And the Lord said, let us make man in our image, and let him have dominion over everything" (Genesis 1:26). When God declared man's dominion, He also proclaimed his kingship. There is a king inside every man, created when God breathed life into Adam.

The Bible declares that human dominion over all creatures on Earth was originally granted by God. However, this authority was lost due to Adam's disobedience, subsequently allowing Satan to become the ruler of the world. In response, God sought a godly individual who adheres to His principles to restore rightful governance.

King Saul, a towering figure, did not follow the *David Principle*. He stood at least a foot taller than everyone else in his kingdom, which made him an intimidating presence on the battlefield. Known for his height and prowess, he struck fear into enemies and earned the title "Saul, killer of thousands." His confidence inspired his men, leading them to victory without defeat. Saul seemed invincible, until Goliath appeared.

Goliath was a terrifying adversary, whose height and stature were unmatched. For the first time in Saul's life, he faced an opponent he could not intimidate by his own presence. Due to his towering height, Goliath was able to look down upon his opponents, instilling fear in them. King Saul was no exception. Twice daily for 40 days, in the morning and evening, Goliath, the Philistine champion, challenged Saul to send forth his own champion to confront him. However, Saul refrained from responding, driven by fear.

Because their leader was fearful, the men who followed him also felt fear. Although Saul was outwardly tall, he internally struggled with anxiety.

Physical stature does not necessarily translate to inner bravery, so when confronted with Goliath, Saul sought someone else to confront the challenge on his behalf. Initially, no one volunteered, until David came forward.

David, although not physically imposing, is known for establishing what I call the *David Principle*. He was of small stature, rugged, and handsome, and unlike King Saul, he had experience in facing larger adversaries. David exemplifies that fearlessness does not stem from physical size but rather from the depth of one's faith in God. He consistently credited his successes to his faith in God, and it was this unwavering belief that rendered him invincible.

Before facing Goliath, David expressed gratitude to God for granting him the courage and strength to overcome challenges such as the lion and the bear. His faith in God fortified his confidence that he would likewise be victorious against Goliath. Consequently, when David was informed of Goliath's challenge to Israel and his curse upon God, he willingly accepted the confrontation.

The confrontation between David and Goliath exemplified the David Principle. The encounter was anticipated to be momentous, with the setting in place. Goliath, a formidable figure equipped with substantial armor, a sword, and a javelin, faced David, a young individual armed only with a slingshot and unwavering faith in God. As they approached one another, their differences became increasingly apparent.

Goliath's attack involved cursing David by his gods, whereas David's approach emphasized his belief that victory was attainable through faith in his God. David proclaimed, "This day the Lord will deliver you into my hand, and I will strike you down; and I will give the dead bodies of the host of the Philistines this day to the birds of the air and to the wild beasts of the earth; that all the earth may know that there is a God in Israel, and that all this assembly may know that God saves not with sword and spear; for the battle is God's, and he will give you into our hand" (1 Samuel 17:46-47 ESV).

Describing this as a battle is an exaggeration, given that it concluded almost as soon as it commenced. David fearlessly ran towards Goliath, launching a stone that struck his forehead. Goliath fell, and David used his sword to cut off his head. The Philistines fled, pursued by the Israelites as far as Gath.

David took Goliath's sword and shield, placing them in his tent, and carried Goliath's head to Jerusalem. The head served as a reminder to the Israelites of the David Principle: that true strength resides within. As stated in 1 John 4:4 (KJV), "Ye are of God, little children, and have overcome them: because greater is he that is in you, than he that is in the world." With a single swing of the sword, a giant was defeated, and a kingdom was restored.

The Fear Factor:
The Proximity Principle (P2)

The *Proximity Principle* states that being close to the source increases power. "For God hath not given us the spirit of fear; but of power, and of love, and of a sound mind" (2 Timothy 1:7). Fear contributed to man's fall, but God provides strength instead. Despite opposition, man can trust in God. Philippians 2:13 says, "For it is God who works in you to will and to act in order to fulfill his good purpose." David's victory over Goliath shows God's work within, providing the ability for triumph. David was fearless and restored God's authority over the kingdom.

Fear arises from the absence of God's presence. Prior to the entrance of sin, Adam confidently walked in God's presence. Regular communion with God boosted Adam's confidence and sense of self, enabling him to handle any task without difficulty. Adam found joy in his labor due to being in the Creator's presence, where joy abounds. However, sin disrupted this connection, resulting in a loss of confidence and self-assurance for Adam. Without God's guidance, Adam experienced further decline; his faith was replaced by fear of God.

Fear opposes faith and impacts the male ego. Away from God, fear leads men to focus on themselves. While self-centeredness can insult God, the male ego's original intent was divine. When God granted man dominion, He gave him the confidence and faith needed to fulfill his purpose.

Adam demonstrated that a healthy ego allowed him to live without fear and maintain regular communion with God. Conversely, when his ego was damaged by sin, he lost faith and withdrew from God's presence. Similarly, today's society has numerous individuals with wounded egos who are distancing themselves from spiritual connection. To positively influence these individuals, we must practice the *Proximity Principle* by maintaining our own connection to God. Additionally, it is essential to assist those within our influence in reconnecting and staying close to Him.

The Ego Factor: The Confidence Principle (P3)

The *Confidence Principle* suggests that a man's self-confidence increases as he gets closer to God, reflecting a clearer image of God to others. According to this concept, the male ego is an indicator of his connection to God and aligns with the *Proximity Principle*. Thus, the male ego itself may not be problematic, but how it is perceived can be. If it is criticized, a man may struggle to become "whole" because damaging his self-assurance in God impacts his overall confidence. Conversely, reinforcing his belief in God can positively affect his self-esteem. The *Confidence Principle* is always relevant to a man's self-esteem. Understanding the ego factor in the restoration process involves several steps.

The male ego was an intentional creation by God. The dictionary defines ego as a person's self-esteem or self-importance, representing his self-image or self-confidence. God's declaration that man should have dominion is the blueprint for his ego. Adam was given the ability to fulfill God's mandate, requiring intact self-confidence. Man's original purpose was dominance on earth, spoken by God and believed by man, benefiting the world. The male ego reflects the *Confidence Principle*.

The creation of the male ego is a direct reflection of God's image. Adam, formed in God's likeness, naturally reflected attributes like power, confidence, and strength. His strong self-image was maintained through his connection with God, as their meetings reinforced his self-assurance. If Adam stayed close to God, he continued to reflect His image. Disconnecting from God would diminish his God-confidence and increase self-reliance. To mirror God's image, a man must stay connected to Him.

We must recognize that the male ego is rooted in the belief that God is the source of all goodness. When God breathed life into Adam, he was endowed with power and wisdom. "Then the LORD God formed a man from the dust of the ground and breathed into his nostrils the breath of life, and the man became a living being" (Genesis 2:7). This divine breath enabled Adam to understand creation, manage Eden, name animals, and perform various tasks effortlessly.

It is essential to understand that the development of the male ego embodies "the lion within," which serves as the foundational source of a man's confident demeanor. Despite his formidable stature, Goliath's self-confidence could not surpass David's healthy ego, which was fortified by his faith in God. Adam fearlessly traversed the garden with confidence due to his strong connection with God; his faith was profound, and his courage was evident. The *Confidence Principle* aims to reflect God's image to the world, serving as the core purpose of the male ego.

The Power Factor: The Lion Principle (P4)

The *Lion Principle* suggests that a person has the potential for power, represented by an inner lion ready to be unleashed. When God breathed life into Man, he became a living being. Through his breath (Spirit), God endowed man with attributes necessary for power and strength. Adam received direct instruction from God, providing him with tools to exercise dominion. Adam's strength and power would be linked to his primary purpose, requiring God's assistance to manage them. Without control, his ego might lead him away from God, resulting in misuse of power and strength. However, when a person's confidence comes from

God, their inner lion is seen as being under divine authority, and the *Lion Principle* is fully effective.

First, the *Lion Principle* asserts that man must be the ruler of his territory. God granted Adam authority over the earth, allowing him to control, guide, and influence others. This divine power was limitless, enabling Adam to exercise control and protection within his environment. Receiving daily instructions from God, Adam named every animal, defining their purpose and demonstrating his unmatched influence in the earthly realm.

Secondly, the *Lion Principle* emphasizes the manifestation of divine strength in man. The breath of God endowed mankind with extraordinary physical capabilities. Despite the reduction in Adam's lifespan due to sin, he still lived for 930 years, indicating that humanity retained considerable power even in a diminished state. Samson, a descendant of Adam, exemplified this strength by performing feats such as lifting an iron gate and tearing apart a lion with his bare hands. However, Samson's story also illustrates that physical strength alone is insufficient; it wanes when one becomes estranged from divine guidance. Therefore, sustained strength and power are contingent upon a man's relationship with God. The Apostle Paul, in the book of Ephesians, advises men to be strong in the Lord and rely on His might.

Thirdly, the *Lion Principle* ensures a man's power is controlled by his ego, which acts as an internal regulator. His ego reflects his relationship with God and is fueled by divine knowledge. Wisdom from God enhances a man's intellectual capacity and humility, preventing self-destruction. The Bible states that men are destroyed due to a lack of knowledge. When connected to God, a man's ego is whole, and his power and strength are under control.

Finally, the *Lion Principle* emphasizes the importance of remaining connected to Christ. It proposes that a man's strength is derived from this connection, and staying connected is essential for maintaining his abilities. Consider John 15:5, which states, "I am the vine; you are the branches. If you remain in me and I in you, you will bear much fruit; apart from me, you can do nothing." According to this scripture, disconnection from God leads to a decrease in strength and capability. This disconnection may result in self-worth being tied to external achievements, potentially leading to dissatisfaction. The *Lion Principle* points out that optimal performance comes from maintaining this connection.

The God Factor:
The Expert Principle (P5)

Wilt thou be made whole? (John 5:6 KJV)

The *Expert Principle* suggests that the creator is the foremost authority and primary source of information about what he creates. This principle indicates that success resides not in the efforts of the individual, but within the wisdom of the Creator (God). In the context of restoring the male ego, the *Expert Principle* advocates for a "factory recall" when issues are so severe that only the manufacturer can repair them. A man who humbles himself before God and allows Him to reset his heart, soul, spirit, and mind to their original state will lead a life of completeness and infinite possibilities. The restoration of the male ego begins with God, as He possesses the expert knowledge required to restore it.

To begin with, spiritual guidance in our restoration efforts is essential, as divine wisdom mitigates frustration. In our endeavors to assist those within our influence, it is crucial to seek wisdom and knowledge from God. The Apostle James emphasizes, "If any of you lacks wisdom, you should ask God, who gives generously to all without finding fault, and it will be given to you" (James 1:5). This scripture is applicable not only to individuals but also to those involved in supportive ministries.

The *Expert Principle* deems that daily interactions with God are necessary because human complexity cannot be fully understood by others. A person's life is full of combinations and variables, making self-teaching ineffective. Imagine a student forgetting his locker combination; repeated failures only damage his confidence. Success requires returning to the creator of the combination. Similarly, God created man and is the only one capable of accessing a man's heart and transforming his life.

The *Expert Principle* believes that God, as the creator, is the best teacher. Failure in teaching leads to disappointment and further failure. Only God knows the right mix for human success and must be central to any plan for positively impacting lives. Jesus taught his disciples to be fishers of men, showing his role as the master-teacher. Following His instructions, they found even devils were subject to them. The *Expert Principle* sees God as crucial in restoring male ego.

Affirmation Factor:
The Gideon Principle (P6)

The *Gideon Principle* proposes that we should acknowledge a person's potential rather than focusing on their issues. It asserts that all individuals require some level of affirmation. Since life can be challenging for those who are broken or wounded, some people have learned to bolster their egos to conceal their shortcomings. Others have become adept at "covering up," using their appearance, speech, or actions as part of the facade. This approach is ineffective and exacerbates the problem. Consider Gideon's story in Judges Chapter 6-8, where the Israelites faced severe oppression from the Midianites, forcing them to live in caves. This oppressive lifestyle was demoralizing for Gideon.

When Gideon is first introduced, he is found living inside a winepress grinding wheat to conceal it from the enemy. This humiliating situation was distressing to Gideon, yet he felt incapable of making any changes. Additionally, his pride was deeply wounded, causing him to harbor anger and place blame on God for his circumstances. Rather than taking offense at Gideon's anger, God took decisive action to restore Gideon's confidence. It is my belief that God recognized the positive qualities within Gideon, and thus, Gideon's misplaced anger did not prevent God from helping.

God sends an angel to affirm Gideon's greatness, saying "The Lord is with thee thou mighty man of valor" (Judges 6:12). Despite initial disbelief, Gideon needed this affirmation. The *Gideon Principle* suggests that affirmation doesn't need approval from the receiver and may face resistance initially. God understood this yet still affirmed Gideon. This conversation was life-changing, stirring up Gideon's buried fearless confidence.

Gideon's self-confidence was damaged, although he retained his strength, power, and intellect. Strength and courage are essential qualities for an individual to be utilized by God. Later, when God sends Gideon into battle, He instructs him not to select those who are weak and cowardly. Similarly, Jesus chose not to select fearful and unbelieving individuals as his disciples, opting instead for the resolute Peter and naming the spirited James and John the Sons of Thunder. Even in today's difficult circumstances, God's restorative power remains available, and God can utilize those who are broken and wounded rather than those who are weak and cowardly.

Ultimately, God affirmed Gideon's sense of self-worth by reassuring him of the trust placed in him. Gideon's realization that God still intended to use him at his lowest point was transformative. As stated in Judges 6:14, "The Lord turned to him and said, go in the strength you have and save Israel out of Midian's hand. Am I not sending you?" God conveyed to Gideon a message of empowerment, emphasizing that despite his current anger, he possessed the ability and strength to overcome the adversary threatening him and his family. This call to action promised success. The restoration of a man's ego begins when he can hear and respond to God's voice; this is the essence of the *Gideon Principle*, which is fundamentally rooted in faith.

The Faith Factor: Gideon Principle-Part II (P7)

Gideon Principle-Part II put forward that fear and faith cannot coexist. Faith is influenced by one's focus, and Gideon's triumph commenced when he redirected his attention from the Midianites to God. As Gideon concentrated more on God, he became increasingly powerful and confident. With his strength, power, and ego intact, Gideon was prepared to confront the adversary. When faith emerges, fear diminishes. Fear is considered the antithesis of faith and results from focusing on challenges rather than on God.

Matthew Chapter 14 illustrates this concept with the story of Peter walking on water. Peter succeeded in walking on water while his focus was on Jesus; however, when he shifted his attention to the wind and waves, he began to sink. This principle applies universally, suggesting that individuals should shift their focus from fears to faith in God. "What I feared has come upon me; what I dreaded has happened to me" (Job 3:25).

Faith comes from experience. The book of Hebrews says faith is the substance of hope and the evidence of unseen things. Gideon's faith was rooted in knowing God directed him. Initially, Gideon didn't recognize the prophet as an angel in human form. Judges 6:22 states, "When Gideon realized it was the angel of the Lord, he exclaimed, 'Alas, Sovereign Lord! I have seen the angel of the Lord face to face!'" This encounter strengthened Gideon's belief that he was indeed a mighty man of valor.

Faith changes one's perspective. For Gideon and his family, hiding in caves would end as God, through Gideon's faith, was about to provide a permanent solution. Remediation means remedying something, especially environmental damage. Every man must seek God's help for restoration, as He alone has the power to fully restore one's rightful place. With Gideon's ego restored, temporary relief turned into permanent victory. Following God's direction with just 300 men, Gideon defeated the Midian army. Gideon exemplifies God's restorative power.

Faith makes God an ally. The God factor is crucial in restoring the male ego, making men fearless and courageous. They see God as an ally and take actions to improve their situation. Faith and ego work together, empowering men to succeed. With restored ego, they view themselves as leaders, embracing their God-given strength and power.

Faith revives the lion within us. Gideon exemplifies God's authority and kingship. When he reconnected with God, he became courageous and took back what belonged to God, defeating thousands with just 300 men. We can also reconnect with God, conquer our inner enemies, and reclaim our families, churches, and communities.

Finally, faith in God mends broken relationships. The adverse effects of fractured relationships, absentee fathers, repressive environments, job scarcity, and dysfunctional governments are evident among contemporary men. However, these challenges are insignificant compared to the absence of a relationship with Jesus Christ. Without divine guidance, Gideon might have remained in despair, and David would not have overcome Goliath. Their faith and application of godly principles were crucial determinants. The restoration of the male ego is dependent on reconnecting with the King of Kings. "Therefore, if anyone is in Christ, the new creation has come: The old has gone, the new is here!" (2 Corinthians 5:17)

.

Chapter 5 Summary

Central Thought – Man was created to have dominion over everything

And the Lord said, let us make man in our image, and let him have dominion over everything. (Genesis 1:26)

Key Discussion Points

➢ Discuss the seven principles to the restoration of the male ego *(P1-P7)*

➢ When a man is connected to God, his ego is full of God-confidence and fear not a factor

➢ David defeated Goliath and proved that the giant within will always defeat the giant without

➢ Acknowledging a person's potential is essential to helping them improve, and this involves speaking to the qualities they possess.

Action Step

Encourage and affirm the men and young men in your environment by looking beyond their current actions and speaking to their potential. For those who have a relationship with God, pray that He will awaken their inner strength. For those who do not yet have a connection with God, pray for their acceptance of Jesus as their personal savior, followed by prayers for God to awaken their inner strength.

The art of Winning
Men to Christ

..and he that winneth souls is wise (Proverb 11:30 KJV)

The friend of the bridegroom

It is the bridegroom who gets the bride, yet the bridegroom's friend, who merely stands by and listens for him, is overjoyed to hear the bridegroom's voice. (John 3:29 ISV)

In John 3:29, John the Baptist uses the relationship between the bride, bridegroom, and the friend of the bridegroom to explain his relationship to Jesus and the disciples. John referred to himself as the friend of Jesus, expressing happiness when the disciples came to Jesus for baptism. John acknowledged that Jesus was the one who came to take away the sins of the world, stating that salvation is possible only through Jesus. John's role, as he saw it, was to guide his disciples to Jesus and feel contentment. Today, the concept continues as individuals consider themselves the "friend of the bridegroom," guiding others towards Christ.

In the lives of contemporary men, as a friend of the bridegroom, we have an important role to fulfil. For many of us, executing this role will necessitate tools, skills, and talents that may not be within our current capabilities. Even for those who possess these attributes, they might not be structured in a manner that is reproducible or measurable. This chapter aims to provide the insight required to win men to Christ and to positively impact their lives. Winning men to Christ must be the primary objective, as it is written: "What does it profit a man to gain the whole world and lose his soul" (Mark 8:36). As friends of the bridegroom, our mission is straightforward—bring them to Jesus and rejoice! This is how we can help the men of today.

What is help? What is enabling? The distinction can be unclear when interacting with individuals in our lives. While supporting someone requires knowledge, it also entails the courage to acknowledge those who are not ready for change. For example, in John 6:26, 66, Jesus ceased providing food to followers and instead offered Himself as the bread of life, leading some to stop following Him. Similarly, Matthew 25 describes five foolish virgins who were unprepared for the bridegroom's arrival. This chapter provides specific solutions aimed at identifying individuals committed to making lasting changes. Additionally, it offers practical tools to effectively support them.

The friend of the bridegroom is aware that there is an art to guiding individuals towards Christ. Proverbs 11:30 indicates that winning souls requires wisdom, which is increasingly relevant in contemporary times. Many men today experience various forms of brokenness, with some perceiving their emotional or spiritual damage as irreparable. The traditional methods may no longer suffice for meaningful engagement. It is imperative for families, churches, and communities to be equipped with modern tools and skills to facilitate men's journey towards a fulfilling relationship with Jesus Christ.

The primary objective of the church and individuals should be to guide people towards Christ. Our responsibility is to introduce them to Jesus and celebrate; He will then take care of the rest. Jesus further clarifies the role of the bridegroom by instructing us to go forth and educate all nations, making disciples of people. While the opportunity is abundant, bringing individuals to Christ can be challenging. To facilitate this process, it can be useful to categorize individuals into two groups: those who approach you and those whom you seek out. As a supporter of the bridegroom, you can celebrate because the bridegroom (Jesus) has arrived.

Winning the men that come to you

"And all who were distressed or indebted or discontented rallied around him (David), and he became their leader. About four hundred men were with him" (1 Samuel 22:2).

Men will approach you because there is a significant need for spiritual guidance, and some of these individuals will enter your sphere of influence. Like the men who came to David, they may not arrive in optimal condition. These men came with great potential but also carried various issues. Some were troubled, others were in debt, and many were discontented. The individuals today are comparable; many come with financial difficulties, wounded pride, broken spirits, and weary souls. They often originate from fragmented families, weakened churches, and unsafe communities. To bring them to Christ, a deliberate and intentional strategy is necessary. Below are four essential steps to consider.

Step 1: See all men as having the potential for greatness

To help individuals reach their full potential, it is important to view them as capable of growth and development. Potential refers to the capacity to develop into something more in the future. What you currently see may not be indicative of what they can become. Because every individual has inherent abilities, what is visible on the surface may not reflect the potential within. For example, 400 individuals joined a group led by David, despite all of them having various issues. Nevertheless, David successfully led and managed them.

David recognized that every individual possesses the potential for greatness. This inherent capacity leads to opportunities for development and growth. Potential necessitates patience and continuous improvement. If one tries to prematurely differentiate between those who are promising and those who are not, they risk overlooking future excellence. Regardless of their initial appearances, David saw the potential in all the men who came to him and treated them accordingly. Four hundred men approached him, and he embraced each one, thereby creating four hundred opportunities for greatness.

David also recognized that potential leads to power. A difference in potential generates power. In electronics, electrons move from negative to positive, and this movement produces the power required to start a vehicle. Without movement, there is no power. When individuals bring forth their potential, one must be sufficiently energized to create the force necessary to direct them positively. Much like electrons in a battery, as they transition from negative to positive, energy is generated. This power can be transferred to others, which led to David's fellowship expanding rapidly from 400 to 600 men. This demonstrates the principle that the more individuals are positively influenced, the greater the potential for future growth.

David eventually realized that power leads to increased capacity. When an individual is endowed with divine power, not only will others be attracted to them, but they will also bring additional individuals along. The Apostle Peter was not originally a follower of Jesus; he came to Jesus because his brother Andrew introduced him. As stated in John 1:42, "The first thing Andrew did was to find his brother Simon (Peter) and tell him, 'We have found the Messiah (that is, the Christ).' And he brought him to Jesus."

Similarly, the Apostle Nathanael was brought to Jesus by another person. "Philip, like Andrew and Peter, was from the town of Bethsaida. Philip found Nathanael and told him, 'We have found the one Moses wrote about in the Law, and about whom the prophets also wrote—Jesus of Nazareth, the son of Joseph'" (John 1:45). When individuals are empowered in Christ, their power and potential are amplified, attracting others to them.

Step 2: Invest in them before you make demands on them

To effectively influence the lives of men and guide them towards spiritual growth, it is essential to invest in them before making any demands. In my book, *"Men are Dirt,"* I describe men as soil that yields more than what is sown into it. Without sowing into them, nothing can be reaped. David's followers were financially destitute and emotionally broken, so he invested in them by offering a safe environment for healing. Providing a space for recovery is one of the most valuable gifts you can offer. Without making any immediate demands, David offered leadership, protection, provisions, and the opportunity for his followers to become self-reliant. He leveraged his power and influence to improve their circumstances and enhance their future prospects.

Leaders identify potential. Under David's leadership, the group began to understand their capabilities. Despite being distressed, indebted, and discontented, David saw them as skilled warriors. They were also brave. David continued to support them, which helped their confidence grow and their self-esteem improve. Gradually, they reached a point where they contributed positively to David's efforts. David nurtured them, leading to their eventual success. With David's guidance and encouragement, they never experienced defeat or lack again.

Effective leaders empower others. In John 14:12, it is stated, "Very truly I tell you, whoever believes in me will do the works I have been doing, and they will do even greater things than these, because I am going to the Father." Jesus instilled greatness in his disciples and delegated power to them. He provided them with authority over demonic spirits, enabled them to feed thousands, miraculously paid Peter's taxes, healed their family members, facilitated their travel, and sent the Holy Spirit to support them in His absence. Additionally, He healed their emotional wounds and restored their self-esteem. Through His resurrection, Jesus empowered them to go forth and teach all nations, assuring them of His continuous presence until the end of time. The same empowerment is available to us today.

Leaders cultivate future leaders. By investing in individuals, you inherently nurture the development of potential future leaders. This principle was evident in my ministry. In 1990, as a young pastor at the age of 28, I had a dedicated group of men seeking my guidance. Without imposing any demands, I committed to their improvement by first ensuring they had a personal relationship with Jesus Christ. Additionally, I vowed to support them and offer protection. Finally, I shared all my knowledge generously, offering my assistance, emotional support, and intellectual resources. These individuals were highly receptive, and many became pastors or achieved even greater accomplishments. The transfer of power through knowledge, guidance, and prayer invariably fosters leadership.

Step 3: Lead others to action

Leaders must take decisive action. To fully leverage the capabilities of individuals within your sphere, as a leader, it is essential to engage all members actively.

When individuals are inactive, they tend to become stagnant, disengaged, and immobile. Greatness cannot emerge from individuals who have been sidelined. Power is derived from actions.

According to Newton's law of motion, an object at rest remains at rest unless influenced by an external force. Transitioning from potential energy to kinetic energy necessitates power. Kinetic energy is dynamic and mobile, akin to a locomotive. It may start slowly, but as it continues to gain momentum, it becomes an unstoppable force. By engaging all individuals within your sphere, their full potential and kinetic energy can be harnessed effectively.

Leaders create motion. According to Newton's First Law of Motion, individuals at rest will remain at rest until an external force compels them to act. The identity of the external force that motivates people to take action can vary. For the men who joined David, he was the catalyst that activated them. As their leader, David exhibited confidence in his beliefs and was proactive. Consequently, the men under his leadership were required to be active as well. David had three basic requirements: first, that they be courageous, second, that they trust his leadership, and third, that they respect God's appointed leaders. For these men, David was the necessary external force to guide them toward restoration.

Leaders play a crucial role in providing direction. According to Newton's first law, an object in motion remains in motion with constant speed and uniform direction. This suggests that a moving object will maintain its course unless influenced otherwise; hence, leadership provides this necessary guidance. The leader's words not only motivate individuals but also ensure collective movement towards the desired goal. David's leadership exemplified this principle, transforming 400 individual men into a cohesive and formidable force. Under his command, they consistently achieved victory without suffering any defeats.

Leaders unlock potential. Jesus empowered all 12 disciples, including Judas. By doing so, He recognized Peter's spontaneity, James' thunderous personality, and John's beloved nature. Empowering those around you reveals their natural traits, helping assign roles that leverage their unique skills. Despite concerns about "one bad apple," don't let fear of a "Judas" prevent you from discovering a "Peter." Use your influence to guide individuals to their intended roles, maximizing their abilities.

Step 4: Promote based on proven performance

The fourth and final step to achieving success in leadership is to promote individuals based on proven performance. There is a difference between activating individuals and elevating them. Activation applies to everyone, but promotions must be earned through demonstrated capability. Rewarding poor performance or no performance sets a low standard that diminishes the value of achievements. If rewards are not deserved, they can encourage undesirable behavior. This principle applies throughout life, from childhood to adulthood. When individuals are promoted based on family relationships, financial status, or friendship, they may not meet the necessary standards for their roles, which can negatively impact the group. Consistent, faithful service should be a requirement, and all promotions should be earned.

The Apostle Paul conveyed the idea that promotion is earned when he wrote, "Now it is required that those who have been given a trust must prove faithful" (1 Corinthians 4:2 NIV). David followed this principle, using faithful service and demonstrated performance as criteria for promoting his men. While 400 men came to him, only 37 showed the necessary qualities to become part of his bodyguards. The closer they were to David's inner circle, the more was expected of them. 2 Samuel 23:8-17 describes the three men who were so reliable and accomplished that they became his chief leaders, with one of them defeating 800 men in a single battle.

To win them to Christ, you must be wise. Men will come to you, but many will be wounded and broken. Invest in them before you make demands on them and see them all as having potential. Activate them all and promote only based on proven performance. David used these principles to take men that were distressed and in debt to be the greatest fighting force in biblical history! Finding greatness requires an expectation of greatness and an environment that fosters it. Power produces power, and great leaders produce great leaders!

Winning the men that you seek out

Not all individuals will approach you. There will be instances where you must actively seek them out. In the scriptures, Prophet Samuel sought out David, and Barnabas went looking for Saul of Tarsus (later known as Apostle Paul). God has a plan for everyone, and certain individuals will enter your life to assist you in achieving it. Whether you are a pastor or a parent, there will be occasions when you will need to reach out to someone to help you attain greatness. This requires a distinct set of skills, as the manner in which you engage with those you seek out must differ from how you interact with those who come to you voluntarily. Here are three steps to consider.

Step 1: Know what you are looking for

To effectively recruit the individuals you are seeking, it is essential to have a clear understanding of your objectives. This approach differs from attracting those who come to you spontaneously; when approaching them, you are targeting specific profiles. Jesus demonstrated intentionality when he sought out Peter and Andrew. Upon encountering them, he stated, "Come, and I will make you fishers of men." Jesus was aware that he needed fishermen for his mission. In contrast, when Jesus visited the residences of Matthew and Zacchaeus, he was not searching for fishermen; rather, He sought individuals with influence.

Secondly, to ensure that you are seeking the right individuals, it is important to have a clear understanding of your purpose. Understanding one's goals allows one to seek people who can support them. For example, a leader who understands their organization's needs will seek out individuals who can help achieve objectives. Similarly, parents who are aware of their needs will look for people with the appropriate skills and talents. Purpose determines needs. One does not seek out a doctor to build a house or a farmer to prepare for a marathon. Knowing what you are looking for helps to be intentional about whom you seek out.

Thirdly, to effectively utilize individuals, it is essential to align their roles with their specific skills and abilities. For instance, fishers should be assigned fishing tasks, singers to singing, teachers to teaching, and accountants to accounting. Each person possesses a unique talent that should be recognized and appropriately employed. Jesus demonstrated this principle by understanding the individual nature of each person, as it is within the heart where one's passion resides. As stated in Luke 6:45, "A good man brings forth good things out of the good stored up in his heart, and an evil man brings forth evil things out of the evil stored up in his heart. For the mouth speaks what the heart is full of." The more knowledge one has about an individual's characteristics, the better they can harness their skills and talents.

Finally, in order to engage effectively with the individuals you seek, it is essential to ascertain whether their aspirations and passions align with your mission. A person's passion often reflects their purpose, and comprehending this purpose can provide valuable insight into their character. While immature individuals may speak impulsively, mature individuals articulate their thoughts with sincerity. By attentively listening to a person discuss their dreams and passions, you can evaluate if they are compatible with your goals. If they are, consider yourself fortunate. If not, it may be prudent to allow them to pursue opportunities that better match their interests. It is worth noting that not everyone within Jesus's broader circle was part of His inner circle. As stated in Matthew 22:14, "Many are called but few are chosen."

Step 2: Defend publicly; correct privately

To support men in leadership roles, protect them publicly and correct them privately. The male ego is fragile, so defending them when they're attacked reassures them of your protection. This isn't about right or wrong; it's about confidence. When men know they're protected, they can pursue greatness without fearing their mistakes will be judged. Public failures should prioritize protection over correction.

Public correction can harm a person's ego, and it goes against the principle that protection should precede correction. It is important to avoid publicly correcting those within our sphere of influence. Jesus demonstrated this through His actions. There were instances when outsiders criticized His disciples, including valid cases where they were challenged for not washing their hands ceremonially, eating food picked from the fields on the Sabbath, and not having enough faith to heal a sick boy. Despite these valid criticisms, Jesus defended them publicly in each case. Publicly supporting individuals under one's leadership does not imply condoning their behavior.

Public correction should not be the initial response in any situation. In the ninth chapter of Mark, Jesus encountered a crowd harassing His disciples due to their unsuccessful attempt to heal a sick child. Before understanding the specifics of the situation, Jesus's immediate reaction was to protect His disciples. He commanded the crowd to cease their harassment. While Jesus did not excuse the disciples' actions, He recognized the importance of correcting them privately at a later time. Although there may be occasions where public correction is necessary, it should remain an exception rather than a standard practice.

Private correction enhances the relationship. Correction is necessary for everyone, and typically, it should be done behind closed doors. Jesus followed up with his disciples in private to bolster their confidence. After learning about the situation, He healed the boy, then took His disciples aside to speak to them. This included providing encouragement and addressing their unbelief. Jesus also advised them that through prayer and fasting, they could handle similar situations in the future. In this private setting, Jesus improved their relationship, addressed their unbelief, and maintained their dignity.

In summary, it is advisable to avoid public correction as it can damage relationships. Protecting someone's self-esteem is important for their spiritual and emotional well-being. Public protection and private correction can positively impact relationships. For example, Mark 4:34 indicates that open communication with the public was done through parables, while private explanations were given to disciples. Public criticism can create fear, whereas private guidance can strengthen relationships.

Step 3: Share the wealth

The third and final step to attracting the men you seek is ensuring mutual success. Similar to how the head cannot be elevated without raising the entire body, your progress must benefit others as well. You should strive to be the "rising tide that lifts all ships." As you advance, those around you should also experience growth. When you receive blessings, those within your sphere should equally reflect those benefits. This principle, rooted in spiritual doctrine, is illustrated in Genesis 12:3 where God promises Abraham, "I will bless those who bless you." It is imperative that individuals who contribute to your purpose share in your achievements.

Many individuals have benefited from the support of others in their lives. When they move on to higher positions, it is important to consider promoting those who have been instrumental in their success. When David ascended to his throne, he brought along the men who had supported him; thirty-seven of them became his bodyguards and lived near the palace. They experienced the advantages of being under effective leadership. Similarly, it is crucial to acknowledge and support those who have helped us advance to the next level.

The principle of uplifting others was evident in the actions of Jesus Christ. He publicly acknowledged his loyal supporters, stating that those who sacrificed much in support of Him would be rewarded a hundredfold in this life and receive eternal life in the next. Jesus assured his disciples that he was not abandoning them but was going to prepare a place for them so that they could be with Him. As Jesus ascended, His disciples became key figures in the church, their followers became bishops, and subsequent generations continued this legacy. Jesus, as the head of the church, was elevated, and consequently, the church body was elevated along with Him.

Strong leaders inspire others

In summary, individuals generally seek to be part of something greater, and effective leadership requires making necessary adjustments while adhering to key principles. These principles include knowing what you are looking for, utilizing people according to their abilities, defending them publicly, providing constructive feedback privately, and supporting their growth. Adhering to these principles will encourage individuals to remain committed and potentially recruit others. Strong leadership continues to inspire and connect people to the things that align with their aspirations and interests.

Everyone has the ability to support others, guiding them to find their path and celebrating their progress. We all know individuals in our lives who are struggling and could benefit from compassion and understanding. Look for opportunities to offer support and share positive words. There are always examples of people whose lives have dramatically improved after receiving help and guidance. This illustrates that everyone is more than what they appear to be.

Finally, if there are challenges in gaining men's participation, adjustments should be considered. Understanding them is essential, requiring recognition of their identities and goals. If your objectives align with their interests, they may remain engaged. When this occurs, the focus should shift to maintaining their activity and engagement. Keeping individuals busy involves understanding who you are and your principles. The next chapter will discuss how character and personal values can be crucial in maintaining active and engaged participation.

Chapter 6 Summary

Central Thought – To win souls, we must be wise

> *It is the bridegroom who gets the bride, yet the bridegroom's friend, who merely stands by and listens for him, is overjoyed to hear the bridegroom's voice. (John 3:29 ISV)*

Key Discussion Points

➤ Supporters of a man's return to Christ are truly "friends of the bridegroom."

➤ The practice of leading individuals to faith in Christ necessitates an understanding of various methods for effective outreach

➤ To maintain a healthy relationship, offer support publicly and address issues privately

Action Step

Cultivate the practice of being supportive by acknowledging and celebrating the achievements of others. Avoid using these moments to promote your own accomplishments or diminish the success of others. Simply listen attentively to their success stories and express sincere and genuine happiness and excitement for their achievements.

Strategies for Maintaining Engagement and Activity

As Iron sharpens iron, so one person sharpens another. (Proverbs 27:17)

Five principles to keeping men active

From this time many of his disciples turned back and no longer followed him. "You do not want to leave too, do you?" Jesus asked the Twelve. Simon Peter answered him, "Lord, to whom shall we go? You have the words of eternal life. We have come to believe and to know that you are the Holy One of God." (John 6:66-68)

It is insufficient to merely convert men to Christ; it is imperative to keep them engaged in the family, ministry, and community. Sustaining active participation among men presents a considerable challenge. Men, by nature, are inclined towards action and their physiology is geared for movement. They tend to become uninterested with monotony or inactivity, therefore passive roles are not a sustainable solution. Engaging men and leveraging their inherent abilities is pivotal in this process, yet additional measures are required.

Keeping men active in any group is largely the responsibility of the leader. Leaders should acknowledge their role in the participation levels of their followers. It is insufficient to simply point out the shortcomings of individuals and ask them to improve; they must be guided towards improvement. The qualities of the leader are crucial in influencing whether followers remain committed. If a leader is limited and self-serving, followers may not stay engaged. Conversely, if a leader is dedicated, fearless, and service-oriented, followers are likely to remain committed. Effective leaders often inspire their followers with a clear vision. While the task can be challenging, here are five principles to help keep members active in your organization.

Principle 1: The leader must humble himself before the Lord

Self-appointed leadership is ineffective in the kingdom of God. Any individual who does not adhere to God's plan for family structure will ultimately fail. When a man humbles himself and submits to God's authority, the Lord elevates him, prompting others to follow. As stated in Joshua 4:14, "That day the LORD exalted Joshua in the sight of all Israel; and they stood in awe of him all the days of his life, just as they had stood in awe of Moses." Joshua did not elevate himself; it was the act of God. God's elevation of Joshua resulted in men willingly following him throughout his life. This willingness to follow cannot be achieved through force or coercion. The individual must humble himself before God to be lifted by Him. When God elevates an individual, others are inclined to follow.

Joshua's humility led to his distinction by God. The dictionary defines distinction as a quality of excellence that sets someone apart from others. Joshua was a leader notable for his honor, greatness, excellence, and glory, qualities bestowed upon him by God. According to Matthew 22:12, those who exalt themselves will be humbled, while those who humble themselves before God will be exalted. This humility must be evident and observable. Unlike King Saul, who concealed his humility, King David demonstrated his humility through his unwavering public confidence in God. As stated in 1 Samuel 17:45, "David said to the Philistine, 'You come against me with sword and spear and javelin, but I come against you in the name of the LORD Almighty, the God of the armies of Israel, whom you have defied.'"

Excellence should be the cornerstone of leadership. It is the distinguishing factor that sets a leader apart from others. Upon elevation by God, it is imperative for the leader to uphold this standard. As stated in Daniel 6:3 (ESV), "Then this Daniel became distinguished above all the other high officials and satraps, because an excellent spirit was in him. And the king planned to set him over the whole kingdom." While men lead families, support communities, and participate in churches, they strive for excellence. In the eyes of God, humility is synonymous with excellence, as it allows the Lord to guide the leader's actions.

Principle 2: The leader must provide a clear vision and mission statement

The need for a vision and mission statement was evident when I began my first pastoral role at a small church in Okinawa, Japan. The congregation consisted primarily of individuals from various branches of the military, representing diverse geographic and religious backgrounds. To foster unity, it was important to provide the church with a clear vision of its direction and a mission outlining how to achieve this aim. These statements would play a crucial role in maintaining engagement and participation among the members.

Men seek direction from leaders, wanting to know where they are headed. Followers need assurance that they are on the right path, as blindly following can lead to cult-like behavior and harm relationships. Sharing a vision helps sustain these relationships. As stated in

Proverbs 29:18, without vision, people perish, but those who adhere to God's word find happiness. True happiness requires divine insight.

Secondly, it is essential for men to understand their tasks and goals (mission) as this is crucial for retaining engagement. In the film *The Karate Kid,* there is a notable scene where the boy, despite following instructions, was prepared to give up because he did not understand the purpose of his actions. He struggled to connect his efforts with the overall mission. To prevent his resignation, the instructor clarified that his actions were not in vain but rather an integral part of his development. The instructor demonstrated patience and provided clarity regarding the results of his work. With a comprehensive understanding of his tasks, the boy continued his journey willingly.

Finally, men often seek clarity on how they can contribute to a mission. When Jesus asked His disciples to follow Him, He provided them with a clear purpose: "And he said to them, Follow me, and I will make you fishers of men" (Matthew 4:19). This purpose guided them throughout their lives, as they followed Jesus until His death and continued after His resurrection and ascension. Post-ascension, they continued to engage in evangelism. A clear purpose generally contributes to a sustained commitment. Connecting an individual's actions and intentions to a well-defined purpose can foster ongoing dedication.

Principle 3: The Leader must be able to lead through adversity

At one point in his life, King David faced a perilous situation. After the Philistines declined his offer to assist them in battle, David returned home to discover their town had been burned and their women and children taken captive. David and his men were deeply distressed. The situation worsened when David overheard his men discussing the possibility of stoning him. "David was greatly distressed; for the people spoke of stoning him, because the soul of all the people was grieved, every man for his sons and for his daughters" (1 Samuel 30:6a KJV). However, David found strength and encouragement in the LORD his God" (1 Samuel 30:6b KJV).

David recognized that his distress was affecting the morale of the troops, so he sought guidance for encouragement. This does not imply that one must hide their emotions or pretend to be happy. David experienced heartache, but he transitioned from a period of grief to a period of strength. With encouragement and support, he and his men pursued the enemy and recovered all. Life is unpredictable, with various challenges and obstacles. Effective leaders must navigate difficult times and lead through adversity. To achieve this, leaders should possess resilience and determination.

Leadership during adversity is essential. All leaders must seek effective strategies during difficult times.

Historical figures have stood firm in the face of great challenges. Although every leader will experience periods of grief, they must follow it up with a season of strength. The leader's response to adversity will directly impact the morale of the people and affect the strength of the family, organization, and community.

Principle 4: The leader must be transparent in organizational affairs

Informed individuals tend to remain engaged. While transparency must be carefully balanced with considerations of who, what, and when, it remains an essential aspect of a leader's communication style. Ineffective communication channels can hinder retention efforts within ministry settings. Secrecy fosters distrust, and misinformation causes confusion. These issues can be mitigated through clear and transparent communication. The same principles apply to family and community environments.

Transparency is the quality of being see-through or allowing light to pass through so that objects on the other side can be clearly perceived. It functions as an essential aspect of vision. As stated in Habakkuk 2:2, "Write the vision; make it plain on tablets, so he may run who reads it." A clear vision and mission statement serve as a vital tool for transparency, enabling the reader to fully grasp and act upon it. Leaders who do not communicate their vision are likely to lack transparency in other areas. Similarly, parents committed to raising healthy, well-balanced children will tend to be more transparent in various family matters. The connection between vision and transparency is applicable across different contexts including work, church, and community settings.

People cannot operate effectively without proper information. Jesus highlighted the importance of transparency, which strengthened his connection with his followers. As stated in John 15:15, "Jesus called his disciples friends because he shared everything his Father told him." In a professional setting, individuals in one's inner circle should be regarded more highly than merely as employer or employee. It is the responsibility of each person to decide the degree of inclusion. However, withholding information can lead individuals to seek clarity elsewhere.

Principle 5: The leader must be able to ask for help

A leader can request essential supporters to remain rather than depart. Some individuals play a crucial role in the journey, and like Hobab was to Moses, they may provide valuable insights (Numbers 10:31). Despite their intentions to leave, it is reasonable to ask them to stay. Reasons for departure may include a feeling of completion, a sense of being unwelcome, or uncertainty about current developments. Requesting them to stay offers an opportunity to address their concerns and initiate a dialogue about their reasons for considering leaving.

Firstly, some individuals might merely be contemplating leaving before they take action; this allows the leader time to inquire about their intentions. Jesus took the initiative to question his disciples regarding their plans to depart, asking, "You do not want to leave too, do you?" (John 6:67). At a time when many were leaving, Jesus demonstrated the courage to ascertain whether his disciples intended to follow the crowd. His questions compelled them to reflect on their commitment to the cause. Peter responded on behalf of the group, affirming that there was no alternative source for words that lead to eternal life. Although some individuals may consider following the crowd, a single word from the leader can alter their course.

Secondly, some individuals may have decided to leave, and out of consideration for you, they will inform you of their plans. In Numbers chapter 10, Moses's brother-in-law Hobab informed him of his intention to return to his hometown. Moses did not accept this as final. He acknowledged that Hobab had been very helpful to him "like eyes to us in the wilderness," and he requested him to stay. "But Moses said, please do not leave us. You know where we should camp in the wilderness, and you can be our eyes" (Numbers 10:31). Following Moses's request, Hobab stayed. Even if those who are assisting you on your journey inform you of their plans to depart, consider acknowledging their contributions and ask them to remain. They might reconsider and continue to support you.

Some men have left, but this isn't the final say. While the leader may not be at fault, it is their duty to bring them back if they are vital to the mission. Consider Saul (later Apostle Paul), who was known for arresting Christians. This made Jerusalem disciples hesitant to meet him. Barnabas arranged a meeting with church leaders, after which Saul preached in Jerusalem until threats forced him to return to Tarsus. When Barnabas learned of his departure, he found Saul and brought him to Antioch to help preach (Acts 11:26).

Seeing men as more than their past failures

In conclusion, maintaining activity among men can be challenging. For some individuals, past setbacks may deter them from pursuing future opportunities; however, it is essential for all men to remain active to stay engaged. When Jesus recognized that Peter was considering quitting due to his public denial, He approached him directly. Unlike certain leaders, Jesus instructed Peter to demonstrate his love by tending to His lambs (John 21:15). This straightforward guidance reinvigorated Peter and restored his confidence in God.

Jesus perceived Peter as more than his past failures and recognized his potential to continue the ministry. Keeping men engaged is also about restoration because if we discard those who are broken and wounded, there will be no one left to utilize. Seeking out individuals who have fallen by the wayside and reintegrating them not only restores these individuals but also encourages those who are already engaged. When engaged men witness others being restored, it reassures them that if they falter, their leader, family, church, and community will assist in restoring them to their rightful place.

Chapter 7 Summary

Central Thought – Keeping men active is not an easy task

Simon Peter answered him, "Lord, to whom shall we go? You have the words of eternal life. We have come to believe and to know that you are the Holy One of God." (John 6:68)

Key Discussion Points

➢ Maintaining engagement among men is a challenging endeavor, which hinges more on the leadership than on the individuals themselves

➢ Every leader should aspire to excellence, as exceptional individuals are inspired by exemplary leadership

➢ A clear vision and mission statement is essential for maintaining engagement and motivation among individuals

➢ The vision statement will define the purpose and rationale behind our actions

Action Step

If you are a leader, create or revise your vision and mission statement to include plans for reaching men. Be transparent, humble, and focused. Emphasize the "why" over the "what," as it holds the power. Evaluate current activities to ensure alignment with your updated statements.

Why chase the Lion?

Be watchful, stand firm in the faith, <u>act like men</u>, be strong. Let all that you do be done in love. (1 Corinthians 16: 13-14 ESV)

The anatomy of the lion chaser

There are three things that are stately in their stride, four that move with stately bearing: a lion, mighty among beasts, who retreats before nothing; (Proverbs 30:29-30)

❝ There was also Benaiah son of Jehoiada, a valiant warrior from Kabzeel. He did many heroic deeds, which included killing two champions of Moab. Another time, on a snowy day, <u>he chased a lion</u> down into a pit and killed it" (2 Samuel 23:20 NLT). "When the image of a man-eating beast travels through the optic nerve and into the visual cortex, the brain sends the body a simple but urgent message: run away! This is the typical reaction;

109

however, lion chasers see differently. They perceive not a five-hundred-pound problem, but rather an opportunity for divine intervention to demonstrate power," Mark Batterson – *Chase the Lion*. Mark Batterson interprets the phrase "Chase the Lion" as a call to cease living with the aim of merely arriving safely at death. He asserts that our aspirations should be daunting and substantial enough that achieving them without God would be impossible.

The motivation behind Benaiah's pursuit of the lion might have been quite personal. It is plausible that the lion's activity on a snowy day indicated it was searching for food. Although the lion fled upon encountering the resolute Benaiah, his family and friends would not have been as fortunate. To safeguard them, Benaiah chose to chase the lion. Utilizing the tracks left in the snow, Benaiah followed the lion into its pit and eliminated the threat, thereby ensuring no further danger to his family and loved ones.

The concept of chasing the lion symbolizes the determination within a person to fulfill their responsibilities as a protector and supporter. When a father is present, it brings a sense of security to the household, yet vigilance is necessary as adversaries may attempt to catch us off guard. In the New Testament, the term "watch" commonly translates from two Greek words (gregoreuo and agrupneo), both meaning to stay awake or to be sleepless. These terms convey the importance of being spiritually vigilant, fully awake, aware, alert, and focused. As stated in 1 Thessalonians 5:6, "Therefore let us not sleep, as others do; but let us watch and be sober."

Like Benaiah, men today are called to protect their families, which is their purpose. At eighteen, this was highlighted for me in *Article I of the Code of Conduct*: "I am an American, fighting in the forces which guard my country and our way of life. I am prepared to give my life in their defense." As a Marine, I saw this oath as a commitment to protect my family, even at the cost of my own life. Paul echoed this sentiment in 1st Corinthians 16:13, urging men to guard their families with courage and strength: "Be on your guard; stand firm in the faith; be courageous; be strong."

Regrettably, the absentee father has disengaged and neglected his responsibilities. This individual is failing to fulfill his duties. His lack of involvement and presence in the lives of his family weakens him, puts his family at risk, and hinders his ability to fully appreciate his blessings, as his children are indeed his blessings. As stated in Psalm 127:4-5, "Like arrows in the hand of a warrior, so are children born in one's youth. Blessed is the man whose quiver is full of them." A man's family should serve as his motivation to remain vigilant and guard them against all threats, be they foreign, domestic, natural, or spiritual. Protecting his family is the purpose that will bring out the best in a man, and like Benaiah, this individual will not retreat under any circumstances.

From lambs to lions

"Rise and rise again until lambs become lions."
– Robin Hood the Movie, 2010

Not all men are aware of their inner strength, but when it is awakened, they can become very determined. "Be brave, Philistines! Fight like men, or we will become slaves to the Hebrews, just as they were our slaves. So fight like men!" (1 Samuel 4:9 GNT). This was the rallying call that went throughout the camp of the Philistines after they heard that the Ark of the Covenant was brought into the camp of the Israelites. The call to "fight like men" motivated them and gave them the strength to defeat the Israelites and capture the Ark of the Covenant. The quote "rise and rise again until lambs become lions" encourages perseverance. As leaders, we must continue to encourage men to fulfill their roles as protectors over their families. Here are some key biblical principles on how to inspire men to develop their inner strength.

First, individuals demonstrate growth when they become mature in their speech. Words are influential. According to John 6:63, Jesus mentioned that his words were full of spirit and life. As words can be life-giving, it is important for a person's words to be thoughtful, intentional, and purposeful. These aspects should be considered before speaking since one's words reflect their level of maturity. While children may speak without thinking, adults consider their words carefully. Immature individuals tend to say immature things, whereas mature individuals say mature things. A person's maturity is reflected in their speech, indicating a progression from lamb to lion.

Secondly, men transition from lambs to lions when they establish their thoughts. Children's "pretend play" shapes their actions but limits their alignment in the real world. A boy who continues to pretend may grow into a man with a fabricated identity. Proverbs 23 warns of men whose words don't match their true thoughts. Mature men base their thoughts on God's word, avoiding being led by imagination.

Thirdly, individuals evolve from being lambs to lions when they become open to redirection. This indicates their ability to reason and be reasonable. The term unreasonable refers to behavior that is not guided by or based on good sense. It is challenging to reason with a two-year-old because the capacity to be redirected develops with maturity. According to Paul, when he was a child, he reasoned like a child, making decisions based on immature thinking. As an adult, he reasoned like a mature person because he adopted more advanced ways of thinking. Immature individuals are difficult to reason with, but mature individuals are capable of being redirected.

Ultimately, men transition from lambs to lions when they accept their responsibility to guide their families. These men are observant, steadfast in their beliefs, and act with care, taking on leadership roles in various aspects of life. This demands vigilance, faith, empathy, and resilience. They draw strength from their principles and values. Their actions are driven by compassion and integrity. They speak transparently and consistently uphold their words. They outgrow youthful behaviors and willingly embrace maturity, taking on family responsibilities. This is how individuals evolve into strong leaders.

As bold as a lion

"Be strong and courageous. Do not be afraid or terrified because of them, for the LORD your God goes with you; he will never leave you nor forsake you" (Deuteronomy 31:6). This scripture illustrates God's expectations for men. Without strength and courage, individuals may become fearful and withdraw. For God, strength and courage are intertwined. Being strong yet cowardly or courageous yet weak does not adequately reflect God's presence in a man's life. The divine influence within a man endows him with strength, while inherent boldness grants him courage. His ego, symbolizing fearless confidence in God, is essential to dispel fear. Consequently, this individual will remain unafraid.

To begin with, this individual will not experience fear of others. God instructed Moses not to be afraid or dismayed by those before him, assuring him that He would always be with him. This divine reassurance significantly influenced Moses's self-perception. As individuals, we require God's reassurance to maintain our confidence. Since our strength is derived from Him, our courage and confidence are closely tied to our relationship with God. "Have I not commanded you? Be strong and courageous. Do not be afraid; do not be discouraged, for the LORD your God will be with you wherever you go" (Joshua 1:9).

Next, this man will not fear demons. When Elisha's servant felt fear due to what he saw, Elisha prayed for God to open his eyes so he could see into the spiritual realm. "And Elisha prayed, 'Open his eyes, Lord, so that he may see.' Then the Lord opened the servant's eyes, and he looked and saw the hills full of horses and chariots of fire all around Elisha" (2 Kings 6:17). Elisha's servant did not know that assistance was already present, and he was fearful because of it. It is suggested that man's inability to walk by faith instead of sight can lead to fear. However, through faith, seeing as God sees, it is believed he will no longer be afraid.

Thirdly, this man will never operate under the fear of inadequacy. As Jesus stated, "I am the vine; you are the branches. If you remain in me and I in you, you will bear much fruit; apart from me, you can do nothing" (John 15:5). Fellowship with God through Jesus fortifies an individual because God is the source of their strength. It is imperative that one does not become self-reliant. Although the branch provides strength and nourishment to the fruit, the ground (God) is the actual source. Just as a plant removed from the soil perishes, so does an individual disconnected from God. While this individual may feel inadequate, Jesus assured his followers that those who continue to abide in Him will be productive and yield significant results.

Finally, this man will no longer fear being unprotected. Roman 6:16 advises us to take up the shield of faith. The Roman shield, known as the scutum, differs from the conventional shield we typically envision. It was a very large, slightly curved rectangular shield with a prominent metal knob at its center. Due to its substantial size (over three feet tall and three feet wide), it afforded soldiers considerable protection from their adversaries. When one "takes up" his shield of faith, he deliberately and intentionally places his trust in what God has provided, even without physical evidence. This individual believes that God exists and rewards those who diligently seek Him. Consequently, this person possesses the boldness of a lion and does not fear others, demons, or his own shortcomings. This individual is fearless!

The lamb and the lion

Be watchful, stand firm in the faith, act like men, be strong. Let all that you do be done in love.(1 Corinthians 16: 13-14 ESV)

Man must remember that he has both a lion and a lamb within him. The lion symbolizes fearless confidence in God, whereas the lamb represents the love and peace of God. As stated in 1 John 4:7 (CEV), "Love comes from God, and when we love each other, it shows we have been given new life. We are now God's children, and we know him." The Bible consistently commands us to love, indicating that love is the evidence of our renewed life and a crucial indicator of our connection to God. According to John, it is our duty to love one another. The presence of the lamb—a humble and submissive spirit—is essential for fostering the peace and love of God.

The lamb exemplifies our identity as God's children. Jesus provided his disciples with a new directive to love one another: "A new commandment I give you: Love one another. As I have loved you, so also you must love one another" (John 13:34). The restoration of male self-esteem reinstates a man's ability to love. Jesus instructs men to love because He has instilled love within them. He informs his disciples that they are connected to Him through their mutual display of affection. Jesus intentionally imparted His love to them, enabling them to love one another.

The lamb demonstrates that we have been restored. It is often said that when much is given, much is required; however, if an individual is broken internally, they will be unable to exhibit love and peace externally. Their words and actions will be influenced by their internal state. As stated in Luke 6:45, "The good person out of the good treasure of the heart produces good, and the evil person out of evil treasure produces evil; for it is out of the abundance of the heart that the mouth speaks."

According to Luke 4:18, Jesus came to heal those with broken hearts. He restores the broken heart and enables individuals to love others as God loves them. An individual's ability to demonstrate godly love to others is a significant indicator that their soul and ego have been restored.

The lamb exemplifies the intrinsic greatness within a man. Love serves as an insightful tool, similar to an x-ray machine, enabling others to perceive the core of a person's character. Without love, a person becomes akin to a clanging symbol that produces noise rather than harmonious music. Love infuses life with significance and externally reflects internal transformation. It is profound and reveals greatness, serving as a genuine measure of God's benevolence. As stated in 1 Corinthians 13:13, "And now these three remain: faith, hope, and love. But the greatest of these is love."

Ultimately, a man must embody both the lion and lamb. Although numerous principles have been shared, there is a single common factor: man. A man will always be central to his life's equation. Despite various influences and efforts to restore the male ego, a man must act independently. Manhood is not defined by age, height, or wealth but by being watchful, faithful, strong, and loving. Such a man achieves a balance between his lion and lamb and finds unity with Christ. Through his relationship with Jesus Christ, he regains his sense of leadership and restores his ego. The restoration of the male ego involves reclaiming our sons and winning our fathers to Christ!

Chapter 8 Summary

Central Thought – Why chase the lion?

Rise and rise again until lambs become lions.
– Robin Hood the Movie, 2010

Key Discussion Points

➢ When men awaken the lion within, they fight like warriors and accomplish the impossible

➢ When God awakens the lion within, the man can function without fear and chase the lion

➢ Both the lion and the lamb exist inside of a man

➢ The lion is man's fearless confidence in God

➢ The lamb is the peace and the love of God

Action Step

Continue to rise and rise again until lambs become lions by never give up on your efforts to impact the lives of men. Each word of affirmation, call for accountability, or introduction to Christ contributes to the overarching plan of God. One person may plant, another may water, but it is always God who facilitates growth. However, your role is essential and invaluable in this process as we strive to reclaim our sons and win our fathers to Christ. Amen.

ABOUT THE AUTHOR

Tim Houston is a husband, father, author, minister, motivational speaker, and entrepreneur. He prioritizes his relationship with Jesus Christ and advocates for a balanced life over a simplistic one, valuing family and friends above fame and fortune. Tim is the proprietor of Houston Publishing and Consulting and possesses substantial experience in both business and Christian leadership.

He has authored two additional books. The first book, *"Study to Be Quiet: Hearing from God During Times of Crisis"*, provides guidance on creating an environment conducive to hearing from God. His second book, *"Men are Dirt: Spiritual Insight for Healthy Relationships"*, offers valuable insights into men from a man's perspective.

Tim, originally from Saginaw, Michigan, now resides in Duluth, Georgia. He places a strong emphasis on family values and, along with his wife Cantrice, is part of a large, blended family consisting of 8 children and 18 grandchildren. For further information about Tim, to schedule speaking engagements, or to obtain copies of his publications, please visit his website.

www.ingramcontent.com/pod-product-compliance
Lightning Source LLC
Chambersburg PA
CBHW050801250626
47155CB00005B/2164